Did a bare foot or leg float somewhere nearby? I expected to see the sleek shadow of a tiger shark turning the far corner of the hallway.

I gained the end of the hallway without meeting any man- or boy-eaters. Seeing Blue Jade's map in my head, I made my way through the dead ship toward the pilot room.

It wasn't hard to find. The door was marked PILOT ROOM. But in the entryway, several feet from the door, lay the one thing I was hoping not to see. Twelve feet of yellow, mucus-covered skin stretched in a sleepy coil, floating inches above the floor. Or above the wall, I mean. The coil ended in a blunt head, with two fierce black eyes, and an open mouth ridged with dozens of flesh-tearing, snaggly teeth. The moray did not move. I was frozen to the spot. Well, as frozen as you can be when you're floating in water.

Be sure to read every Finnegan Zwake Mystery:

The Horizontal Man
The Worm Tunnel
The Ruby Raven
The Viking Claw
The Coral Coffin

Available from Simon & Schuster

THE
C·O·R·A·L
COFFIN

A FINNEGAN ZWAKE MYSTERY

MICHAEL DAHL

SIMON PULSE
NEW YORK LONDON TORONTO SYDNEY SINGAPORE

First Simon Pulse edition January 2002
Text copyright © 2002 Michael Dahl

SIMON PULSE
An imprint of Simon & Schuster
Children's Publishing Division
1230 Avenue of the Americas
New York, NY 10020

Designed by O'Lanso Gabbidon
The text of this book was set in Times Ten.

Printed in the U.S.A.
2 4 6 8 10 9 7 5 3 1

ISBN 978-1-4169-8665-2   ISBN 1-4169-8665-0

Special Thanks are due to Bill Thomas of Charleston, South Carolina, for sharing his scuba-diving expertise and punny good humor; to Becky Kirkpatrick of the Science Museum of Minnesota, for colorful insights on the Great Barrier Reef; to Jon Mikkelsen of the National Theater for Children for his creepy suggestion concerning the blue-ringed octopi; to Mark Ryan, agent extraordinaire; to Ingrid van der Leeden, the most creative editor I've ever met; to editor Samantha Schutz, for always asking the right questions; and, of course, to Danny Thomas, an amazing teacher, and the smartest, kindest man I know.

To James Edward Fairburn—
world traveler, boy wonder.

1
WHAT THE SKELETONS
TOLD US

"Weird lights. They shouldn't be there."

"I don't see any lights," I said.

Uncle Stoppard handed me his binoculars and silently pointed to a low green hump on the turquoise horizon. I knew that whales traveled these waters, the northern tail of Australia's Great Barrier Reef, but this whale didn't move. The high-power binocs morphed the blurry whale's back into a low island, wearing a fringy crown of dark green shadows. Coconut trees. A shore the color of vanilla ice cream belted the trees like a wide, golden welcome mat.

"Weird," repeated Captain Stryke.

"I still don't see any—"

"Off to starboard, Finn," said Captain Stryke.

"That's a little to the left," whispered Uncle Stoppard.

"Thanks for the tip, Uncle Stop," I whispered back.

"Don't mention it," he said. "I know how all this nautical, or shipping, terminology can sound confusing to the beginner."

Before climbing aboard Captain Stryke's ship, the *Forty-Niner*—a weather-beaten sailing vessel painted red and gold for the captain's favorite American football team—I had already memorized some basic boating lingo. During the long flight from Minneapolis to Australia, I had plenty of time to learn that *port*, *starboard*, *bow*, and *stern* meant the left, right, front, and back sides of a ship. That's why I now silently ignored Uncle Stop's advice and trained the binocs a half-inch to my *right*, the starboard side of the coral island. I also flexed my knees, trying to absorb the bobbing of the *Forty-Niner* as I stared through the powerful lenses. Yup. The captain was right. Lights—electric lights—danced weirdly among the trees. The bluish haze of dusk made them easy to spot once you knew where to look.

"That's not a beacon, either," remarked Captain Stryke. "Not supposed to be any beacons in this area."

According to Captain Stryke's charts, the island sitting a mile away from us was deserted, except for stray crabs or sea turtles or flying brown boobies. The blinking, moving lights, however, proved there were humans on Reversal Island. And I knew who they were.

The deck shifted under my sneakers, and I lost my sight line of the island.

Captain Stryke gripped the handrail and tossed a look at the sky. "That's what I was afraid of," he said. Clouds gathered like a thickening soup.

"It was clear a minute ago," said Uncle Stoppard.

"That's the equator for ya," Captain Stryke said.

"An outburst can whip up in five minutes out of nowhere and drop a ton of water on you in half that time."

"An outburst?" I looked at Uncle Stoppard, who shrugged his bony shoulders at me.

"Better head belowdecks," said the captain.

"When can we land on the island?" I asked.

"Depends on Mother Nature," he answered. "It's getting dark, too. We need to find a safe channel through that coral lying between us and the island. I'd prefer if we waited till morning."

"But I've waited a hundred years for this," I said.

"A hundred years?"

"Okay, eight years. But we're so close."

Captain Stryke was quickly lowering the *Forty-Niner*'s main sail. In nautical terminology that sail is called the, uh, mainsail. I was holding on to the handrail with my left hand and trying to get another bead on the island through the binocs in my right. No luck. The *Forty-Niner* swayed like a little kid's rocking horse. Growing waves slapped against the hull.

Uncle Stoppard's complexion matched the cucumber-green of his eyes. His short, spiky red hair looked spikier in the sudden gust of cool wind that blew across the deck. He stumbled next to me, grabbing the handrail.

"Get on down below," said Captain Stryke.

"I'll be in the john," Uncle Stoppard said to me.

"It's called the *head*," I said. More boat lingo.

"Thanks," he said weakly.

"Don't mention it."

He bent his tall frame as he climbed down into

the cabin, but he still knocked his head with a loud thump against the top of the hatch. Just as he did each time he used those stairs. Which explained the glowing constellation of bruises on his forehead, right below his hairline.

I turned back to the horizon. Where had the island gone? The low hump of sand and trees had disappeared behind a gray wall of pouring rain. As the rainwall approached the *Forty-Niner* from the east, the setting sun on the left side of the ship, the port side, threw brilliant bloody light on me and Captain Stryke, decorating us in his favorite football team's colors. His faded baseball cap blazed like a ruby. My white T-shirt burned hot pink. My khaki cargo shorts gleamed like gold.

Captain Stryke pointed to the rainwall. "That's a super wet, that is!" he cried.

Captain Stryke wasn't a real sea captain. He was an ex-police captain from San Francisco back in the U.S. When Uncle Stoppard and I found his red-and-gold sailboat bobbing in the harbor back in Cape York, and when Captain Stryke found out that we were fellow Americans, he told us all about his old job during the three-hour sail out to Reversal Island. What brought him to the northeast corner of Australia, he said, was the peace and quiet and sailing and fishing. What he left behind in San Francisco, he said, were people always shooting each other. I guess people don't shoot each other out on the Pacific Ocean. So why did Captain Stryke tell us that he slept with a pistol under his pillow?

An old habit from his cop days.

Uncle Stoppard and I have an old habit, too. We

keep running into dead bodies. A dead body is what brought me and Uncle Stoppard to Australia in the first place. A skeleton, actually.

Eight years ago my parents handed me over to Uncle Stoppard and then flew off to Iceland. They were searching for the Lost City of Tquuli, an ancient Viking burial city, because they were both archeologists. I mean, *are* archeologists. I mean *both*. They're both alive, but they're considered legally dead since they disappeared from Iceland eight years ago. Their footprints were found on the side of a snow-covered mountain. The footprints ended in the middle of nowhere. So how do I know they're alive?

Several months ago Uncle Stoppard and I flew to Iceland ourselves, retracing my parents' footsteps, hoping to find clues to explain their mysterious disappearance. We found two skeletons. And each bony carcass contained a clue.

On the jawbone of one of the skeletons, my mother (I think) had drawn an ancient rune in bright red lipstick. Runes were the letters of the Viking alphabet. The rune my mother wrote was the symbol for *A* or the "ah" sound. And beneath the rib cage, on the ground, she had written two Icelandic words: *mikill* and *veggur. Mikill* means big, huge, great. *Veggur* means wall or barrier.

See? It all makes sense.

Great.

Barrier.

A for Australia.

My parents were telling us that they were being taken to the Great Barrier Reef of Australia. Who

had taken them, or why, or how, I didn't know yet.
But I knew the answer lay on Reversal Island.

You see, the second clue, on the second skeleton,
was a wristwatch. My father's wristwatch. He had left
it behind on purpose, encircling the bony wrist of the
long-dead Viking, knowing that the modern invention
would be noticed on the ancient arm. The hands of the
watch were set at a specific time. Nine o'clock. Why
nine? It stumped me at first. Even Uncle Stoppard
wasn't sure what my father had meant by that. But
when Uncle Stop and I returned to our home in Minneapolis, it finally dawned on me. It was dawn and a
loud crash woke me instantly from a deep dream.

"Uncle Stoppard! Is that you?"

"H. E. double hockey sticks!" he yelled from the
dim kitchen in our apartment.

"What happened?"

"I pulled the dairy drawer out of the refrigerator
and it fell on my foot."

"The refrigerator?!"

"The dairy drawer."

Uncle Stoppard was always crashing or dinging
or banging some part of his anatomy against a table
or doorway or car window. He continued talking to
himself in the kitchen.

"Where's the shredded mozzarella? Oh, never
mind—I just stepped in it. Hmmmm, I'll bet it's still
okay. I mean, I did take a shower before I went to bed."

I made a mental note to myself: Don't touch the
shredded mozzarella.

Why did Uncle Stoppard yell out that bit about
the hockey sticks?

Uncle Stop explained at breakfast, pressing

three plastic bags of ice against his black-and-blue toes. "It's a habit I picked up from my dad. Instead of yelling a curse word, he always spelled it out. Hockey sticks are shaped like the letter *L,* you know."

Yes, I knew that. What Minnesota kid doesn't recognize a hockey stick?

With the *whoosh* of a Minnesota Wild skater connecting with a skimming puck, it hit me. The clock hands on my father's abandoned wristwatch were not showing the time. They were showing a shape—an L-shape.

I jumped up from the breakfast table, grabbed an atlas from the hall bookcase, and slammed it open to the map of Australia. I scanned all up and down the twisty spine of the Great Barrier Reef, my maple-syrupy finger tracing each island and town along the eastern coast of Australia. From Rockhampton in the south to Cape York at the northern tip I spied for anything that had an *L* sound. Lady Elliot Island. Long Island. Tully, Innisfail, Helenvale. Nothing seemed to fit.

My finger was quickly running out of reef and was heading toward the empty, undotted blue of the Gulf of Papua. Wait, there it was. At the northernmost end of the coral barrier, a tiny black speck. Reversal Island. Reverse L. Of course, that's what the skeleton's wristwatch was telling us. The clockhands showing nine o'clock formed a backward, or reverse, *L.* Dad was a genius.

Uncle Stoppard was stunned at my discovery. His jaw dropped open, which is not a pleasant sight, by the way, when you're eating waffles for breakfast. He exclaimed, "Finn, you're a genius!"

To look at us, you wouldn't think we were related, Uncle Stop and I. He's tall and muscular, I'm short and slender. He has green eyes, red hair, and a long nose (Uncle Stoppard calls it *aquiline*). I have light brown hair, pale skin, and freckles. Uncle Stoppard tells me I have a *mochaccino* mop, *java* eyes, and a *triple-latte* complexion with *nutmeg* sprinkles. Uncle Stoppard likes using big words. He also drinks a lot of coffee.

And because Uncle Stoppard is a famous, award-winning mystery writer (one of those awards was a million bucks), we were able to buy plane tickets to Australia.

What were my dad and mom doing on Reversal Island? I hoped to learn the answer in the next twenty-four hours.

"You'd better get inside if you don't want to get drenched, son!" yelled Captain Stryke.

The rainwall was less than a hundred yards from the deck of the *Forty-Niner*. The shore of Reversal Island was hidden somewhere behind the falling outburst. Earlier, Captain Stryke had told Uncle Stoppard and me, sandwiched in between his cop stories from the streets of San Francisco, that Reversal Island had been given its unusual name by nineteenth-century whalers. A whaling ship had been hit hard by a tropical storm, its masts sheered off, its rowboats flung into the wind. The whalers drifted through the Pacific for several weeks, running low on food and fresh water. Soon they were surrounded by a school of man-eating sharks. Shacks, as the Australians call them. The starving whalers awaited their doom.

One whaler happened to glance out over the water and sighted a small island hanging low on the horizon. After an hour of paddling with broken timbers and ripped-up planks, a quick search of the tiny island revealed a well of fresh water and trees full of juicy mango and coconut. The men's destinies were reversed. Instead of disaster, a second chance. Hence, Reversal Island.

As the captain told us that story on our trip out from Cape York, I wondered what would have happened to the whaling crew if that one whaler hadn't looked up. What if his bleary, fading eyes had missed the island? Or if he *had* seen it, what if he had dismissed it as a mirage or a distant cloud? What if a sudden squall or outburst hid the sandy beach from their vision? The whalers would have drifted out of sight, floating farther away from the Great Barrier Reef, farther from safety, and into the Coral Sea. And eventually into the satisfied bellies of various tiger shacks.

A tiny thing can make a big difference in our lives. A wristwatch, the letter *A*.

Thunder boomed. I stopped thinking about the captain's story, grabbed my backpack from the side of the deck, and headed for the dry safety of the hatch.

Funny. My arms felt weird. I looked down and saw, from my wrists to my elbows, the tiny, mochaccino-colored hairs were all standing straight up. It was like the science trick that Mr. Thomas showed us in fifth grade, when he brought a big aluminum ball into class one day. He called it a Vandergraff generator. He wound up a handle on the side of the device, charged it with static electricity, and told everyone to take turns touching the ball. Everyone's hair stood out like porcupine quills.

I glanced over at Captain Stryke. His snowy white beard, normally smooth and trim, looked like an albino porcupine hanging from his chin.

That was when a bolt of lightning struck the mast of the *Forty-Niner.* Captain Stryke screamed. A blue flash blinded me as the electric charge hurled me backward off the deck of the ship and into the churning waves of the Pacific Ocean.

2
CASTAWAY

Dark water rushed over my head. Silence swallowed up the booms of thunder and the roar of falling rain slamming into the surface of the ocean. I opened my eyes underwater. Blackness surrounded me. On the wavering surface, lightning flashed pools of neon over my head. Fireworks over the water. In one brilliant flash I was surprised by a hulking shadow. A shack. Then I realized it was probably the underside of the *Forty-Niner.*

I pushed myself upward toward the lightning. My head broke through the waves and was dumped on by the rain. Rainfall crackled and sizzled loudly all around me. Where was the ship? I kept flipping my feet, treading water, to stay afloat. I couldn't see the *Forty-Niner.* Suddenly a dark head bobbed up next to me.

"Yow!"

It was my backpack. I must have been holding on to the sack when I was blown off the ship. It bobbed next to me on the water like a fat blue jellyfish.

Luckily I was wearing a life vest. Captain Stryke

insisted that Uncle Stoppard and I wear them for insurance reasons. Boy, was I glad Captain Stryke had insurance. Otherwise my body would be dropping like a brick through the bottomless water. I'd end up like one of the dead bodies in Uncle Stoppard's murder mysteries.

"Hey! Uncle Stoppard!" I shouted. I could not see the ship, but while I was underwater I had seen its shape. It must be close by. The thick curtain of plummeting rain hid it from my view, just as it had hidden Reversal Island from me while I was still on board the *Forty-Niner.* Now all I could see was a gray circle of angry water surrounding me with another ton of water falling straight down on top of my head.

"Uncle Stop!"

Torrents of rain pounded against the surface of the waves, drowning out my yells. I ducked my head under the water again. Quiet and peaceful down here. Rain didn't fall or hiss down here inside the ocean. But the underwater was black as ink. When lightning blazed up above, I had a wider range of vision: schools of ghostly fish darting beneath a ceiling of oily light. Between the flashes, however, I was swimming through black soup. If my glasses hadn't been attached to my head by their elastic safety cord, black soup is all I'd have seen even with the lightning flashes, thanks to my nearsighted eyes.

I couldn't stay underwater for long. The life vest kept dragging me up to the surface like a bubble in a soda pop can.

Again and again I bobbed my head under the water's surface like a Minnesota loon. Lightning flashed off and on. Where was the shadow of the ship? Captain Stryke and Uncle Stoppard must be looking for me. Unless Captain Stryke was also zapped off the deck. That meant Uncle Stoppard was alone on the *Forty-Niner*. He didn't know anything about running a ship. He didn't even know that the starboard side means the right side! The lightning might have fizzled out the ship's electrical power, or melted the engine, or worse: ignited a fire. No, the outburst would drown out any fire.

A huge shape slithered through the dark water. Not the ship. This shape was long and narrow. Like a sea serpent. What the heck was it?

"Hey, Uncle Stop, over here!"

The outburst drizzled away. Thirty minutes after the last drop rolled off the top of my soaked head, it was true night. No stars or moon lit up the sky. Only the occasional lightning flash, moving farther and farther away, lit up the surface of the black, oily sea. The thunder grew fainter. It sounded like the ocean's stomach was rumbling. When I yelled, my voice echoed over the bare, shipless waves.

Should I pick a direction and start swimming? I wondered. I might end up swimming farther away from the ship. Wait a minute. Before the outburst hit, the ship had been a mile away from Reversal Island. I couldn't have drifted that far away from my original position. If I kept my ears sharp, maybe I would hear the sound of waves hitting the Reversal beach. That would give me a definite direction to aim for.

I didn't want to move around a lot in the water. I didn't want to attract attention. On one hand, I heard that shacks, I mean sharks, are attracted to the scent of blood in the water. Gee, I hope I didn't have a scrape or cut on my legs from falling off the ship. On the other hand, I heard that sharks are attracted to movement, a human boy's legs and arms flailing around in the water. On the third hand, I wished I had never seen the movie *Jaws.* Twelve times. Especially that scene where the guy goes to rescue the kids swimming in the canal and—oh, never mind. Why did Uncle Stoppard always rent that stupid video each time I begged him? Why didn't he just say no?

Yeah, right. And he should have ignored me when I insisted we sail on the *Forty-Niner* today. I was a total jerk about it. Captain Stryke had told us up front that the weather was "iffy." But I pushed Uncle Stoppard into sailing today.

"I can't wait!" I said. "It's been eight years, and now we have definite proof that Dad and Mom are on that island. They need our help!" The proof, of course, were the clues left behind on those creepy skeletons in the cave back in Iceland.

Uncle Stoppard is always dogging me about having more patience. Taking my time. Time? I don't have time. I'm already fourteen and life is slipping through my fingers. I've got to find my parents before it's too late. Is that being a jerk? Maybe. When you want something so bad, you forget or ignore everything else around you—is that wrong?

People say, "You waited eight years, what's one more day?" Well, the way I look at it, if you keep saying *What's one more day?*, *What's one more day?*, pretty soon those days add up. The days turn into years, my parents are still missing, and I'm grown-up and ancient like Uncle Stoppard.

There I heard it. Rushing and crashing. To some

ears it might sound like fans yelling at the Super Bowl while doing the wave, or faraway bombs exploding one after the other. But I knew it was a beach. Waves pounding against a vanilla-colored shore.

I struck out in the direction of the crashes. The noise grew louder, but my arms grew tired. My muscles ached when I tried lifting them above the water. I turned over on my back and paddled slowly with my feet. Eventually I would get there. The current should help push me in that direction. Good thing the water near the Equator is warm.

I still held on to my backpack with my right hand. I gazed upward at the sky and kept paddling. At one point I slowly, painfully, groped through the water and removed each of my sneakers, tying them to the vest along with my backpack. I thought bare feet and toes might work better in the water. I took a deep breath. Then it was back on my back and paddle till daybreak.

Clouds.

Clouds, not stars?

The sky was growing lighter. Morning already. The clouds were only wisps of darkness against a darker darkness. As soon as the sun came up, I should be able to see the island. The crashing grew louder with each passing moment, each passing wave, but my head hadn't hit the beach yet. Sounds must travel really far over the surface of the water. In fact, I think my science teacher Mr. Thomas taught something about sound waves in class. I should have paid more attention. Did we study sharks, too? I know Mr. Thomas had the jawbone of a shark. Not in his face; it was suspended over his desk by invisible piano wires. He was given the jaws from a fellow teacher from Florida. He once took down the jaws and let us touch the teeth. Rows and rows of them! Since sharks don't have dentists, each time a tooth gets knocked out from chewing a particularly tough sailor or tourist, another tooth slides into place. Hundreds of sharp, pointy fangs lodged in the yellow jawbones. Like pieces of glass embedded in the top of a cement wall. Mr. Thomas passed the jawbones over the head of one kid and down along his body to his sneakers. Some bite.

The sky turned from black to blue. One edge of the endless ocean burned neon pink. That was east. North was where the crashes came from. I flipped over, got a mouthful of salty Pacific, and started dog-paddling. My muscles ached less. Earlier, it felt as if a Hummer had run over my arms. Now it only felt like a minivan had rolled over me.

A dark shape appeared on the horizon. A blue-green whale-back shape. Reversal Island!

I dog-paddled like a swimmer in the Olympics. The crash of the surf roared in the waterlogged shells of my ears. My mouth and eyes burned with salt water. The scent of exotic, unfamiliar flowers tickled my nose.

Without warning, a pounding wave lifted me up and threw me onto the shore. I landed with a thud.

"Uff dah!"

Firm wet sand greeted my cheeks. Coconut trees, striped with morning light, swayed only a few yards away. Pink clouds sailed high over the island. What was that saying I had heard from Uncle Stoppard?

Red skies at night: a sailor's delight
Red skies at morning: a sailor takes warning.

No need for a warning here. I had finally made it. Now I had to go find my parents.

My knees weren't working. Neither were my elbows. All the joints in my body had turned to rubber. Maybe if I closed my eyes for a few seconds, just a few, and gathered my strength, I could go hunting for my folks in a minute. Two minutes. Okay, make it ten.

I'd go hunting for Uncle Stoppard, too.

And for the *Forty-Niner* . . .

And for Mr. Thomas's science class . . .

And . . .

I fell asleep on the shore of Reversal Island.

3
REVERSAL

A shriek ripped through the bright air.

Not a human shriek, but the scream of some bird or creature hidden within the island forest. The sun blazed in the bright white sky. The sand burned beneath my legs. How long had I been sleeping? Was it already afternoon?

"Yah!" The sand was hot. I jumped up and ran to the cool shade of the nearest trees. Which wasn't easy, considering my legs were half-asleep, and the backpack and sneakers still hanging from my life vest kept banging into my knees. I sank onto soft green grass.

My throat was on fire. I needed drinking water. I hoped the well the old whalers discovered was still working after a hundred years.

From the shade of the trees, I took a first good look at my surroundings. A trio of pelicans flew low out over the water, diving into the waves, and swooping back up with their bucket-like beaks full of dripping fish. The birds flew parallel to the shore, heading to my right, and swiftly disappeared behind the curve of the island. The rest of the horizon was full of sky and water. A darker line of water separated the island from the main body of the ocean. That must be part of the coral reefs. During the boat ride yesterday, Captain Stryke had pointed out the tops of some reefs only a few inches below the ocean's surface. Tourists in this neck of the world enjoy spending part of their vacations walking on the reefs. Pretending they can walk on water. Ha ha. Uncle Stoppard and I had spotted a few reef crawlers while sailing on the *Forty-Niner*.

Captain Stryke had used a few choice words to describe the crawlers. He said they were destroying the reefs, breaking off chunks of delicate, thousand-year-old coral with their clumsy shoes. He had pointed his cigar at the crawlers and said, "How would they like it if some tourist came along and crawled on *their* backs? On the roof of *their* house? Not likely, I'll wager."

Where were Uncle Stoppard and Captain Stryke now? The little red-and-gold ship was nowhere in sight. I was sure that even my bleary eyes would pick out a blob of color bobbing on the blue waves. Nothing in sight except for a few more pelicans and boobies. I could tell the two seabirds apart from their distinct colors, pink and brown.

If Captain Stryke had been blown off the deck of the *Forty-Niner* like I was, maybe he was somewhere on the island, too. He would have heard the waves hitting the shore like I had. With more experience being on the ocean than I had, he surely survived the lightning strike. Uncle Stoppard worried me more. My last sight of him was when he knocked his head against the hatch as he climbed belowdecks to the cabin. Had he hurt himself? He could be lying unconscious on the floor of the ship, oblivious to the lightning bolt, not knowing that he was abandoned, drifting out to sea. Is *floor* what they call the bottom of the ship? I'll have to ask Uncle Stop what the nautical terminology is.

Why hadn't I gone down below earlier? I would have escaped the lightning, stayed on the ship, and seen Uncle Stoppard lying on the floor.

I couldn't worry about that now. As soon as I found Dad and Mom, we'd go hunting for Uncle Stop.

"Hello!" I yelled.

No response.

"Hello?"

I stood up on my aching feet, slipped on my waterlogged sneakers, and started walking. The cool, squishy insides felt good against my hot soles. I figured the whalers' well was most likely inshore, so I headed into the shade of the coconut forest. Tall, leafy palms draped the path with cool shadows. The warm air was full of noises: cawing, shrieking, whistling, singing. A thousand invisible birds surrounded me. A few times I heard a branch snap overhead followed by a flash of brilliant scarlet or emerald green flying through a shaft of sudden sunlight.

The grass gave way to bare dirt in a few places. This was a good sign. Any footpath leading to a source of fresh water was bound to be well-traveled.

"Hello!" I called again.

What was that smell?

Not a flower or fruit. It was cool and delicious and familiar. Water. I ran forward through the tall grass and burst into a small clearing. A pool of perfectly clear water lay before me. Water trickled over rocks surrounding the pool and formed a small stream that wound off through the forest to my right. I plopped down on the grass, held my head above the water, and lapped it up like a dog. Several gallons later I rolled over and sighed. Life was beautiful again.

The grass felt softer than my mattress back home. . . .

Green melons hung from the trees. Were they safe to eat? I wasn't that hungry. I could wait until I found Dad and Mom. They would have plenty of food.

Too bad I didn't have a canteen or thermos to take some water along with me. What happens when I get thirsty again? I propped myself up on my elbows and looked around. The beach gleamed beyond the trees. I made a beeline to the vanilla-colored sand, and when I reached it, I planted a tall stick in the sand, marking the way to the well. If I got thirsty later, if Dad and Mom didn't already know about the well or were low on supplies, we could walk along the beach and eventually find this stick again. One good thing about islands: they only have one shore. If you keep walking you'll end up where you started. Reversal Island didn't look all that big on Captain Stryke's charts. It was a couple miles around. No bigger than some of the lakes back home in Minneapolis.

I must have slept longer than I realized. The skin on the back of my neck and round the bare edges of my T-shirt sleeves felt tender. The backs of my knees were sunburned as well and chafed each time I took a step.

An orange fireball was sinking slowly toward the ocean, four inches above the horizon. Half the sky was growing purple like a bruise. How could the sun be setting already? Had I fallen asleep back at the well? Well, if I kept walking, I'd find my parents.

"Hello!"

Still no answer.

Maybe they were listening to a radio or something and couldn't hear me. I couldn't hear a radio myself. Only the invisible birds calling and chirping and clicking to each other.

Oh, no! The island was smaller than I thought. My footprints lay before me in the sand. I had completely circled Reversal Island.

Wait. These were footprints. Not shoeprints. I was wearing my sneakers. These tracks belonged to someone else, someone not wearing shoes! I slipped my right foot out of my shoe and placed it next to the right footprint. My foot was smaller. An adult was walking on this island. Hey! There was a second set of prints joining the first.

I had found them!

"Mom! Dad!"

My parents and I were circling each other on Reversal Island. Like two radio satellites revolving around the Earth, we were on the same orbit, but opposite sides. Well, Satellite Finn was going to speed up and catch the other one. I decided to turn around and go in the opposite direction. That way we'd be walking toward each other.

The backward prints continued along the upper edge of the beach, staying in the narrow boundary between sand and grass. The sun was sinking. Pink and orange pools burned on the ocean. Gold clouds appeared out of nowhere, pointing toward the sun in long, feathery streaks. Although it would be dark soon, it wouldn't be hard to follow the prints. My ears always knew where the ocean was. As long as I kept the water to my right and the forest to my left I would keep moving forward. Waves crashing in one ear, birds crying in the other. Stereo island.

But no sound of a human voice.

Please, please let me find my parents soon.

Uff. It was getting so dark that I almost tripped over a rock.

Uck. The rock moved. It stuck out its large green snout and clacked its mouth at me. A turtle. No, two turtles. Or was that five?

This section of the beach was studded with hundreds of round rocks, and each rock was alive. The turtles had neon-white circles round their eyes. The tips of their beaks were spotted strawberry-red. They were like amoebas; every few moments it seemed as if the turtles had doubled in number. My sneakers had less and less sand to stand on.

On my right, shimmering on the water, shells glinted with silver moonlight. A herd of turtles—is it herd?—were moving inland from the ocean and marching onto the sand. The beach resembled a giant vibrating pizza; each pepperoni slice had four slimy feet and a tail.

My parents' footprints were destroyed, literally wiped out. Hundreds and hundreds of turtle flippers, crossing and crisscrossing the sand, had obliterated them. What were these stupid reptiles doing anyway? I had to be careful and not run. I knew that some turtles had tough beaks that could tear a nasty wound. Were they poisonous? That's all I needed. A turtle bite and no school nurse nearby.

The dark sky was loaded with stars, twice as many stars as the Minnesota sky. The starlight and moonlight were bright enough to illuminate each rough, shiny shell that surrounded me. Bright enough to keep me moving forward.

Beaks or no beaks, I had to reach my parents.

Cautiously I tiptoed around shell after shell. It was like walking through a minefield where the mines kept moving. Once or twice a particularly grumpy turtle would hiss or threaten me with its gross little jaws, but none of them made an attempt to nip at my ankles. I wondered if any of them had ever seen a human being before?

For being such a gigantic flock of turtles, they were weirdly quiet. A thousand flippers made soft swishing sounds in the sand.

I wonder if my folks had any of these guys for dinner?

As I reached the far end of the turtle minefield, I noticed that the sand the turtles had not crawled on was smooth and empty. The backward footprints I had been following no longer trailed in this direction. My parents must have walked from the forest. The black shadows beneath the coconut trees were noisy with unseen creatures. I stared into that chattery gloom until my eyeballs hurt. No electric lights danced among the trees. My parents were asleep.

What should I do now? It was easy to get lost inside those dark, leafy shadows. A pit or ravine might be waiting for me to stumble in unaware. Or some nocturnal creature bigger and meaner than a turtle. I don't think there are any snakes on the Great Barrier islands. Or bats.

I hate bats.

The evening air was warm and comfortable. As I stood there, not knowing which direction to move, my legs still ached from last night's swim. I sat down on the grass edging the beach, made a pillow of my backpack and life vest, and lay down, staring up at the Pacific stars.

Uncle Stoppard once told me that the smartest move to make is sometimes not to move at all. I sure hoped this was smart, because my muscles were not planning on moving anywhere.

The sounds of the soft, swishing turtle flippers filled the air.

Swish ... swosh ...

I blinked a few times and it was morning. Wow! Swimming takes a lot out of a person. Guess that's why it's an aerobic sport. Now I felt thirsty again, but not as thirsty as I had yesterday. Today, this morning, I was going to find my parents if it killed me.

I stood up and stretched, brushing the sand from my arms. The water closest to the beach glowed a deep blue-green. Except for a few scattered shells and a lonely yellow crab scuttling next to the water-line, the bright vanilla sand seemed vacant. Twenty yards farther down the beach, tossing gently in the surf, a thick pile of seaweed bobbed half-in and half-out of the water.

From the seaweed stuck two human legs.

4

DEAD JOKE

I ran down the beach, yelling like some crazed soccer fan, "Uncle Stoppard!"

When I reached the body, I knelt down and turned it over, stripping off the seaweed. It was a woman. Her shoeless feet lay in the green water. Mom? I brushed long strands of blondish gray hair, matted with sand, away from her face. Ah, I breathed a sigh of relief. Not my mother. Though I have not seen my mother for over eight years, I have her face memorized from a photograph I keep with me at all times. I know that her face will have aged in real time, but I know exactly how she will look. Images of her's and Dad's faces have flashed into my brain every day for the past eight years. Mental snapshots. In my mind, I know every wrinkle, every hair, every square inch of skin.

I did not know this woman on the sand. Maybe she was a friend of Mom and Dad's. Why was she out here on the beach by herself? Her clothes were sand. I mean, sand-colored, as well as covered in sand. A short-sleeve shirt, a vest full of pockets and zippers, knee-length shorts, and a web belt. Sand sprinkled her bare skin like cinnamon on a doughnut. On her right wrist she wore a heavy-duty watch, chronometer I think it's called. A gold ring gleamed on her left hand.

Wrinkles crinkled the ends of her mouth and the corners of her eyes. She looked older than Uncle Stoppard, maybe forty or fifty. She also looked beautiful, movie-star beautiful, if you could ignore her purplish lips.

How did she get here? There were no other footprints around her body except mine. She must have washed up on shore. Had lightning struck her boat, too? In that case, she would have drowned in the storm that night, and her body would have sunk to the bottom of the ocean. It takes several days for a dead body to fill up with gas and then rise to the surface. Then it's called a "floater." Her body was not swollen with gas. It had its natural shape. A beautiful figure. There is no way she could have drowned.

But her purple lips proved she died from lack of oxygen.

I know a lot about dead bodies from Uncle Stoppard, because he's a mystery writer. In our apartment back in Minneapolis, he has a whole shelf in his office crammed full of reference books on how bodies die. Very cool stuff.

It also helps that my family has a thing for dead bodies. My dad's mom, Grandma Zwake, was a paleontologist and devoted her life to sniffing out and digging up dinosaurs. Her bones are on display at the Smithsonian in Washington, D.C. My other grandmother was a spy for the CIA, a spook. My cousin Andy works the graveyard shift at a Tombstone Pizza factory. My cousin Ophelia is the mayor of Kilgore, Nebraska. See? *Kill . . . gore?* My mom's favorite writer is Robert Graves. My dad's favorite band is the Grateful Dead. I like ghost stories and reading about mummies. So I guess you could say dead stuff is in our blood.

Like the doctors in Uncle Stoppard's reference books, I tried out other causes of death. There were no bruises on her body. No blood anywhere. No gunshot wounds in her skin or clothes. (And I've seen gunshot wounds before. Yech.) No signs of strangulation, either. Uncle Stop calls those kinds of signs ligature marks, marks left by a rope or belt on a victim's neck. Bruises may also be left by a killer's fingers and thumbs. But there were no signs of a struggle on this woman.

Was she poisoned? If she had been poisoned on a ship and tossed overboard, she would have sunk to the bottom. If she had been poisoned in the water while swimming, by a jellyfish or something worse, again she would have sunk. Unless a creature stung her in shallow water while she was wading on to the shore. A poisonous sting would have left a mark on her, like a monster mosquito bite. Her skin, however, was smooth and tan.

I glanced out over the water. No sign of the *Forty-Niner* or this woman's ship. I noticed again the green water separated by the coral reef from the dark blue of the farther ocean. The coral reef. I had read there were poisonous creatures in the reef. Uncle Stoppard had bought me a book in a small dockside shop in Cape York titled *Danger Below*. It had great color pics showing the various dangers hiding among coral: box jellyfish, also called sea wasps; tiger sharks; stonefish and firefish with their deadly venom-filled spines; shells that shoot a poisonous quill like a harpoon; the zillion-toothed moray eel. Coral itself is dangerous. If you scrape your skin against the coral, poison can get into your bloodstream.

Wait a minute. Last night, before the outburst, Captain Stryke had said that a wall of coral separated the *Forty-Niner* from Reversal Island. That's why he wanted to make landfall in the morning, so the daylight would help him spy a channel through the barrier. So how did I reach the island? Did a current of water naturally guide me through a channel last night? The coral wall blocking the *Forty-Niner* from Reversal Island lay a mile from the island's shore. The reef that I could make out from this beach was only forty yards away. Was it the same reef? I did not have a good feeling about this.

I didn't have a good feeling about the dead woman, either. Who was she and how did she get here? I looked for clues in the seaweed and sand around her body.

A few inches from her right arm lay a beautiful cone-shaped shell. Five inches long, the shell was a glossy pink, circled with red and brown bands. I reached out to grab it for a better look.

"Don't touch that!"

I was so surprised that I jumped to my feet. A man was running from the shade of the coconut trees toward me and the dead woman.

"Put that down!"

"I didn't even touch it," I said.

"What are you doing out here?"

The young man had a sharp, angular face. Thick dark hair crowned his head. A scar creased the right side of his forehead. I had seen him somewhere before. But how? He was tan like the dead woman. His clothes were similar to hers, too: sandy shirt and shorts and socks. White sneakers protected his feet against the hot beach.

"What are you doing here?" he demanded.

"Nothing," I said. "I mean, I lost my ship. Or, my ship lost me. I'm not supposed to be here. Well, actually I am, but not this early, and not without my uncle and my captain. And my parents. Do you know Anna or Leon Zwake?"

He stared at me as he drew closer. Then he stared at the body.

"Oh, my gosh! Joke." He knelt down quickly and felt for her pulse against the side of her neck. He pointed at the pink glossy shell and whipped an angry look at me. "Did you touch that?"

"I said I didn't. What is it, anyway?"

The guy turned his attention back to the woman. Without looking at me he said, "It's a geography cone. Deadly. It can kill you with one barb of its poison."

I thought the shell had looked familiar. I must have seen its picture in *Danger Below*. Now, where had I seen this guy before?

"Who is she?" I asked.

"Dr. Jocasta Carpenter. We worked together. Our ship—" He sat back, kneeling in the sand, and contemplated the dead body as if it were a statue.

"Lightning?" I asked.

That got his attention. "What? Uh, how did you know?" he asked.

"Same thing with me," I said. "Lightning hit our ship. The *Forty-Niner*. We were coming from Cape York to this island. An outburst turned up suddenly, and lightning hit our mast."

The sharp-faced guy stared more carefully at me. "Did you get burned?" he asked.

"I don't think so."

That's where I had seen this guy. He looked like the guy from *Jaws*. You know, the sheriff. The guy who was afraid of the water but still went after the shark. This guy looked just like him, except younger and more muscular. I think he was upset. He kept staring at poor Dr. Carpenter as if he might burn a hole through her head with his X-ray vision. The doctor's skin was turning pink. A slowly boiling lobster. Flies were buzzing around her bare, wet toes.

"We should move her into the shade," I said. "Out of the sun."

"Okay. Careful of that cone," he added.

The guy grabbed under the doctor's shoulders, and I lifted her ankles. In the hot sun she still felt cold. We stumbled our way across the sand and laid her down on green grass in the shade of the coconut trees.

"Lightning hit your ship, too, huh?" I said.

He knelt down in the grass and nodded. "Yes, lightning. Just as you said. Our ship was hit right before dark."

I looked at the gold ring on the doctor's hand. "Is she your wife?" I asked.

"What? Oh no. We worked together. I was a member of the crew. Joke is one of the world's leading authorities on coral reefs."

"Joke?"

"Her nickname. Joke is short for Jocasta. That's what we all called her."

We? "You mean there's more of you?"

"Five scientists and two crew. I don't know what happened to the others. You and Joke, uh, Dr. Carpenter, are the first people I've seen on the island."

October is springtime below the Equator. According to Uncle Stoppard's guidebooks, the average tropical temperature for Cape York and the northern Barrier Reef for this time of year is 80 degrees. The blazing sunlight on the sand probably upped that temperature by a dozen more notches, but when the *Jaws* guy said "the first people I've seen," a spooky, cold chill ran its fingernail down my backbone. "You haven't met my parents yet?"

"Your parents?" he said. "I thought you were alone."

"Sort of alone."

"Who are you?" he asked.

"Finnegan Zwake. Finn for short. Like Joke. My parents are on this island."

"Zwake, huh?" His eyes shrunk into hard, black raisins. "You accidentally got swept onto this island, but your parents just happen to live here?"

"I was coming here on purpose," I said. "Our ship was going to land here in the morning. The captain wanted to navigate his way through the reef during the daylight."

"What are your parents doing here?" he asked.

"I don't know," I said. "But I know they're here instead of in Iceland."

"Iceland?"

"It's a long story."

The guy glanced down at Dr. Carpenter's body. "Yeah, well, it looks like we're going to have time to hear a long story."

"As soon as we meet my parents, we can get off the island. After we find Uncle Stoppard, of course. My folks must have a ship of their own."

"I didn't see any sign of a ship," said the guy.

No ship? The cold fingernail trailed down my spine again.

"Of course, I've only been on *that* side of the island," he added, jabbing a thumb over his shoulder. "I was on my way to the other side when I saw you." Toward my side, in other words.

There had to be a ship. Or mini-sub. "Reversal Island is, like, hours away from the mainland," I said. "My parents must have a way of getting back there."

"Reversal Island?"

"That's the name of this place."

"Listen, mate. I've been reading sea charts and working on a science ship for the past six months. I'm quite familiar with the name of Reversal Island. And this is not it." He stood up with a grunt, put his hands on his hips, and glanced out at the sapphire water. Then he pointed toward his right, past the curve of the island, in the same direction I had seen the pelicans fly. In the direction of his footprints. "*That's* Reversal Island," he said.

Following the aim of his finger, all I saw was water and blue sky. Then my burning eyes began to focus. A whaleback lifted its dim shape above the horizon. A tiny, low island sat miles away from the vanilla-colored beach where I now stood.

5

MANTA

"You all right, mate?"

Why shouldn't I be all right? The ocean current had carried me miles away from the *Forty-Niner*. Miles from my parents and Uncle Stoppard. If Uncle Stop and Captain Stryke were searching for me, what would lead them in this direction, to this tiny drip of lava-snot in the middle of the Pacific Ocean? The *Jaws*-looking guy must have read my mind.

"Tonight I'm building a bonfire," he said. "Anyone sailing by here at night will see the fire. And during the day the smoke will let people know we're here."

"Yeah."

"Cheer up, mate. We're not that far from civilization," he said. "By the way, my name's Billy. Billy Pengo. Former navigator on the U.S.S. *Manta.*"

The *Manta*?

"You mean as in Journey of the *Manta*?" I asked.

"The same," said Billy.

Cool.

The *Manta* was a high-tech science ship on a

two-year mission to explore the Pacific Ocean. Back in my science class in Minneapolis, we followed the ship's discoveries over the Internet. The ship was electronically connected to schools all over the world, just like the Ann Bancroft expedition to the South Pole. I probably even saw Billy on one of the *Manta*'s digicams.

The *Manta* was the world's most advanced research ship, a "stealth boat." High-tech like a stealth bomber. It had originally been a military ship, then was bought by the fabulously wealthy Ackerberg Institute. The Ackerbergs are the same people who hired my parents and sent them all over the globe on archeological jobs. The Institute transformed the *Manta* into a science ship and fitted her with a crew of scientists from around the world. What made the *Manta* unique was its shape. Most ships are built with curving sides, imitating the shapes of fish and whales. The *Manta* was all angles and sharp edges. It was especially useful for examining whales at close range. Whales have built-in sonar that bounces off normal ships and warns the creatures of nearby humans. The stealth *Manta* is undetectable by sonar and radar: radio waves are broken up by the ship's weird angles and sides.

Whales were not the only subject of the *Manta* team. Billy and Dr. Carpenter, along with four other scientists, and another crewman, had sailed all over the South Pacific exploring islands, coral reefs, and ancient civilizations. I remembered my science teacher Mr. Thomas showing us the *Manta* Web site when the crew had discovered buried artifacts on some tiny, forgotten Hawaiian island. The artifacts were golden knives, called *kris* from the kingdom of Srivijaya. But Srivijaya, in Indonesia, was five thousand miles from Hawaii! The *Manta* discovery made all the newspapers. With the evidence of the kris, the science team had proved that seventh-century sailors had traveled from Indonesia, near Australia, all the way to the middle of the Pacific.

The discovery of the kris had reminded me of my parents' own discoveries when they went on archeological digs. My dad and mom had uncovered golden Maya artifacts in Central America and Viking treasure in Iceland. Gold that went to the mysterious Ackerberg Institute. I wonder what Billy thought of his employers. Had he met those weird agents who dressed totally in black, wearing sunglasses even in the dead of night? When Billy meets my folks, they'll have lots to talk about.

"Wow! Were you with the *Manta* the whole time?" I asked Billy.

"I jumped off after the lightning struck," he said.

"No, I mean when they were sailing around the Pacific," I said. "All those months?"

"I joined them after Hawaii," he said. "The original navigator got sick, and I was the replacement. Lucky me, huh?"

"You don't sound Hawaiian."

Billy laughed. "Good thing, mate. Because I'm from New Zealand."

So maybe I hadn't seen Billy on a digicam. But now that I looked at Dr. Jocasta Carpenter again, her beautiful face of appeared familiar—maybe I had seen her on TV.

"We should bury her," I said.

"That's a good idea, Finn." He wiped the sweat off his forehead with an arm and said, "You should be glad *you* didn't drown out there."

"She didn't drown."

"What?"

"Your friend didn't drown."

For the second time Billy's eyes turned into hard raisins. "Who are you?"

"I know a lot about dead bodies because of my uncle."

"He's a mortician?"

"He's a mystery writer."

"How can you tell that Joke didn't drown?"

I explained how the bodies of drowning victims take several days to surface. There would have to be an autopsy. Maybe the doctors would find some kind of poison in her body. But for now, it was impossible to say exactly how Jocasta Carpenter had died and exactly what caused her lips to turn purple.

"You're telling me she could only have gotten to the shore if she was a—a floater?"

"Or she might have died right after she reached the shore," I said. "But I can't tell how. There are no other footprints or marks around her body. You don't think that cone-thing killed her, do you?"

"The geography cone? They're extremely deadly," said Billy. "But it would leave some kind of inflammation or pustule on her skin."

"Huh?"

"A blister."

My bare hand had been only two inches from that glossy shell when Billy first shouted at me. "I forgot to thank you," I said.

"For what?"

"For telling me not to touch the cone. Lucky you stopped me before I picked it up."

"Lucky is right."

Weird how something so beautiful, like the shiny pink-and-red geography cone, can be so dangerous.

"One stab of its tooth," said Billy, "and an hour later you'd be dead."

"Yow. That little thing has a tooth?"

"More like a harpoon. Tons of little creatures on these reef systems can kill humans," said Billy. "Maybe it's only fair. Humans have been killing the reefs for years."

Finding Dr. Carpenter's body, and then meeting Billy, had made me forget how hungry and thirsty I was.

"Did you find any water on this island?" I asked. My voice came out in a croak. My throat was dry, as if I'd been chewing the beach last night in my sleep.

Billy smiled. "Follow me."

I followed him. I stepped over my backpack and life vest as we continued along the edge of the forest, where the grass and sand mingled, our backs to the distant Reversal Island. In a few moments Billy stopped and pointed. *"Voilà,"* he said.

Two large coconut trees lay on the ground. Looking at blackened sections on their horizontal trunks made me guess that they had been struck by lightning two nights ago. Billy waded into the leafy end of one tree, bent down, then disappeared. I heard a snapping sound. When he emerged, stepping backward out of the palm leaves, he held two large bowling balls, one in each hand. Coconuts.

"This way," he said. We walked a few feet toward a large rock wedged in the sand. He handed me one of the coconuts, then knelt close by the rock. Raising his bowling ball high over his head, he brought it down with a crash against the rock. *Gooosh!* The nut split open, revealing a snowy white interior. "This one's yours," he said, handing me the two halves of the nut. Then he split the second one.

Never have I tasted anything so delicious. I've always liked coconut candy bars, but this was a hundred times better. The coconut milk poured down my throat like liquid moonlight. Thinner than cream, thicker than water, sweeter than white chocolate.

"Don't drink both halves at once," Billy cautioned. "Save something to drink after you've eaten the meat of the coconut."

Good advice. After I bit into the soft, white coconut insides, I got thirsty all over again. I finished my first island breakfast—more like brunch, seeing how late it was getting—with a long, satisfying gulp of milk. Uncle Stoppard would love this stuff.

Billy and I sat in the shadow of a few unfallen trees while he told me, in amazing detail, about the voyage of the *Manta*. The day grew hotter, and I knew that we would need to build that bonfire pretty soon, and bury his friend, but Billy kept chatting and chatting.

"You know what coral is, right?" he asked.

Duh. "Like that stuff out there," I said, waving toward the reef offshore.

"That's only the part of coral you can see. That's the skeleton. The living part of coral are little tubes called polyps."

Polyps, Billy told me, are miniature, microscopic toilet-paper rolls with stinging tentacles waving at one end. A chemical oozes from the polyps and hardens around them like cement, protecting them from predators. The cement—the polyps' external skeleton—is the hard, colorful, rocklike part of the coral that people take photos of. Or walk on. Millions of coral polyps living together, oozing and mixing their chemicals together, make up a single reef. The Great Barrier Reef, made of gazillions of polyps, is the largest living thing that can be seen from outer space.

The Great Reef is made of different types of coral: brain, galaxy, staghorn, red whip, broccoli. And each kind of coral has thousands of little polyps living inside it, like renters inside a fantastic, colorful apartment building. But—and here's the unbelievable part—each small polyp is an apartment building for millions of even smaller plants that live inside *them.* Teeny tiny algae. The algae is called zooxanthellae.

"Zoh zan—?"

"*Thel* ee," Billy sounded out for me. "Zo zan *thel* ee."

"Why do tiny things have such long names?" I asked.

"Makes them feel important."

One square inch of coral can contain six million of the little zozan guys. *Six million!* The coral polyps provide the zozans with protection, while in exchange the busy little zozans give the polyps food, make the actual chemicals that harden into reefs, and stain the coral different colors. Red, purple, orange, yellow. Without the zooxanthellae there would be no Great Barrier Reef. No reefs anywhere.

Billy said that the holes in the ozone layer were heating up the oceans. When the temperature goes up, the ice caps melt, and the water level of the oceans rise. Plus, the water gets warmer. Well, the poor little zooxanthellae are real delicate and can only live inside a certain temperature range. It would be like taking a native Minnesotan from the Boundary Waters and plunking him smack in the middle of the Amazon jungle. Way too much culture shock. What would the Minnesota guy do with all his sweaters and mittens and snowboots? And no more ice fishing. Before he learned which Amazon berries weren't poisonous, or how to catch a tropical fish, the Boundary Waters guy would end up dead from piranhas or something. Same thing with the microscopic zozan plants. If the weather doesn't get back to normal, or the ozone layer doesn't get stronger, the corals will all die.

More than half the corals in the Pacific Ocean are already destroyed.

Guess what else coral reefs do besides look pretty and shelter little islands from rough ocean waves? They make oxygen. Tons more oxygen than those chopped-down trees in the Amazon ever did.

"No zooxanthellae, no oxygen," said Billy. "No oxygen, no us."

We'd all end up deprived of oxygen like poor Dr. Carpenter. That's a lot of purple lips.

"Where's the *Manta* now?" I asked.

Billy hugged his knees and looked out over the greenish water. "At the bottom of the ocean," he said.

"It sank?"

"The lightning hit part of the ship's hull. It cracked open and started to take on water when we all jumped ship."

The Ackerbergs would not be happy about the loss of their stealth ship.

"Were you studying the corals around this island?" I asked.

"We hadn't planned on stopping here. We were on our way from Hawaii to the southern end of the Barrier Reef. But we had an extra day—"

Boom.

Billy jumped to his feet.

"What was that?" I cried.

Boom.

The color had disappeared from Billy's face. He looked sweaty, and not from the heat. He raised a finger to his lips. "Quiet." Then he ran into the forest.

It wasn't easy following him. Billy could run like a white-tailed deer. He scrambled around bushes, sliced through humps of tall grass, hopped over fallen tree trunks, swooped under low branches. At least I had eaten a coconut. Otherwise I would have pooped out and lost Billy in the brush.

Boom.

"What the heck is that?" I said.

Billy spun around with a fierce expression on his sharp face. "Shut up, you idiot!"

Geez, I was just asking a simple question.

Ahead of us, shining blue water glistened between the trunks of the trees. We had reached the other side of the island. As I walked up behind Billy, he shoved me to the dirt. "Get down and stay down," he whispered.

He joined me, then scurried on his belly into a clump of tall grass. I scurried right behind. Peering cautiously through the grass, I saw a much wider stretch of beach than the one we had left in such a hurry. And in the water, twenty feet offshore, rested a ship. The long hull was painted pale blue and blended in nicely with the sky behind it. Very cool camouflage. It was not the *Forty-Niner,* but who cared?

"I knew it," I whispered. "A ship." This must be the quickest rescue on record.

Several men had waded ashore. They were not the Navy. These guys wore regular everyday clothes, some in khaki pants, some in shorts. Sunlight glanced off aluminum shovels carried across their shoulders. A few men carried bags.

Billy's silence was contagious. Normally, I would have yelled something, or rushed down the beach to greet our soon-to-be saviors. But something about Billy's mood got to me. What was going on?

The strange men began digging in the shallow sand. Whatever it was they were after, it didn't take them long to find. They dug a few inches, grabbed something small and white, and stowed it in the bags. These guys were efficient. In a few minutes the beach was dotted with dozens of holes.

"What are they?" I whispered.

"Clown turtles," said Billy.

The men were digging up turtle eggs, huh? That's what all those creatures had been doing on the sand last night: laying eggs. After all their hard work, the poor reptiles would never see their hatchlings. I had never heard of clown turtles before. Maybe they were the turtles that made all the other turtles laugh.

"Um, actually, when I said, *what are they,* I meant those guys," I said. "Who are they?"

Billy did not move a muscle. "Pirates," he said.

6
MOVABLE BODIES

Pirates are supposed to dig up buried treasure, not turtle eggs. Especially *clown* turtle eggs. That's not dangerous. I can't imagine fierce, macho sailors having a sword fight and spilling their blood over a couple dozen Grade-A's. Maybe the eggs were actually hollow and contained jewels or drugs. That would be more like it.

"But how do you—?"

"Sshhhh!"

How did Billy know these guys were pirates? There wasn't a black flag with skull-and-crossbones fluttering over their ship. They didn't have swords tucked into their belts. Not a single wooden peg leg in the bunch. Squinting my eyeballs a little harder, I could pick out what might have been rifles or machine guns slung over their shoulders.

Maybe they weren't pirates at all. Scientists are the kind of people interested in turtle eggs. These guys might work with my parents. My mom and dad could be on that ship.

So why were the egg diggers carrying machine guns?

"When you say pirates—" I began.

"They're coming this way," he said. "Run, Finn!"

Like a frightened cat, Billy climbed over me to escape the egg hunters. He crawled out of the grass, scrambled to his feet, then zipped off through the dense trees. I turned back and saw two of the diggers approaching our clump of grass. Yup, those were machine guns. The men might have been hunting for more places to dig, but I wasn't going to stick around to find out. I raced after the retreating Billy and didn't stop running until I was back at the beach I first met Billy on. He was too fast to keep up with. I leaned against a coconut trunk and gulped in warm air.

Billy was nowhere in sight. To my right, Dr. Carpenter's horizontal figure still lay in the green grass. A breeze brushed the grayish-blond strands across her quiet face. Ash blond, Uncle Stoppard would have called her hair. As I stood there, leaning weakly against the tree trunk and catching my breath, I couldn't help wondering about the doctor's death. Now I knew who she was, but not how she died. Uncle Stoppard says that the right explanation for something is usually the simplest explanation. He calls it Occam's Razor. You cut away all the stuff that doesn't fit, all the way-out theories. Then, once the unimportant or complicated or bizarre ideas are shaved away, the simple truth is all that's left. What was the simple truth behind Dr. Carpenter's purple lips?

My orange life vest and my backpack were lying in the grass a few feet away. I remembered passing them when Billy and I walked to the fallen coconut trees. Maybe that's where Billy was hiding. Mmm, my mouth watered at the thought of another coconut. But what if the so-called pirates came to this side of the island?

Low voices muttered in the bushes behind me. I gave a last glance at the doctor's body, scurried over to my vest and pack, snatched them up and raced off in the direction of the fallen coconut trees.

The voices grew louder. I glanced quickly around. No place to hide, except for the leafy ends of the fallen trees. Those green fronds were thick enough to crouch behind. I rushed over to the same tree where Billy had gathered the coconuts. A body rose up, and backed out of the palms. Billy?

A pirate. A bare-chested man, copper skin glistening, thick black hair tied back with a bright blue bandanna, a rifle slung in a black holster over his shoulders. Our eyes locked. Was my expression as startled as his? I glanced at his empty hands and thought of how Billy had backed out of the leaves earlier. I bent down, picked up two coconuts and lobbed them at the guy. Naturally, he caught them. His hands would be too busy with the coconuts to hold his gun, I hoped. Wrong. The pirate dropped the coconuts and reached for his rifle. Then he yelled something at me. No, he was yelling in pain. One of the coconuts had landed on his bare toes.

I jumped over the fallen trunk and darted into the forest. I expected a bullet to come whizzing past my ear and bury itself in a nearby tree. The pirate must have still been hopping around, holding his foot in his hands. His screams, though, would soon attract his buddies.

Two buddies, to be exact. Standing directly in my path. One of them was already gripping his rifle. He stood at least seven feet tall in a khaki shirt and black shorts, his huge muscular legs as big around as my waist. Like his hopping-mad chum back at the coconuts, he also wore a blue bandanna, knotted around his thick, tree-trunk neck.

The other man on the path was one of the weirdest creatures I've ever seen. He was small for a man, my height, and had short black buzzed hair that stuck up from his head like black bristles on a shoe-brush. His face was young, smooth, and hairless. He also looked muscular, but his body seemed, well, twisted. His face was turned toward his friend, but his chest was aimed at me, while his knees and feet seemed pointed in different directions of the compass. At first I thought maybe he had whipped around to see me, surprised by my appearance in the forest. Then he took a step toward me. His body remained in the same twisted alignment. His feet approached me, while his chest was turned slightly away, and his head was skewed to the opposite side. In fact, when he walked toward me, he had to swivel his head back around to keep his eyes on me. His feet, knees, torso, and face were all screwed around an invisible axle, and none of them lined up with the other. A human mattress coil. A Slinky with bad hair.

A faded blue bandanna circled his forehead. His brown eyes were soft but looked as if they did not miss much.

The bigger guy said something.

"I don't understand," I said.

They spoke to each other in the same language, the big man barking, the twisted guy's voice low and raspy. Chinese? Japanese? Indonesian?

The twisted guy nodded to me. "American?" he said.

"Me? Yeah, I am."

He nodded to his huge companion. The big guy growled a few words, gripping his rifle more tightly. The small, twisted guy put his hand on the other's weapon and said something, like he was calming him down. (I hoped.) Then they had what sounded like an argument. Abruptly they stopped. Their buddy from the coconut tree had joined us, limping down the path.

All three pirates exchanged words, fast and furious.

The twisted guy turned his head around to me and said, "What are you doing here?"

"I got lost," I said. I figured I didn't want to mention Mom and Dad at this point. Or Uncle Stoppard and Captain Stryke. A kid like me was harmless, but an adult would be more of a threat. The pirates might get nervous if they thought there were more people around.

"I, uh, came from Cape York," I continued.

"Cape York, Cape York," they all mumbled.

"Yeah, I was on a boat with some friends and we got caught in a storm."

"The lightning storm," said the twisted guy.

"Right, the outburst. And I fell overboard and landed here."

"You are alone?"

"Yes. I don't know where my friends are."

"The dead person—is that your friend?"

"What? What dead person."

"The dead lady on the beach."

Of course I knew about Dr. Carpenter. But when he said *dead person,* for a picosecond I was afraid he might be referring to another dead body. Billy Pengo. Or some body I hadn't seen yet, on another part of the island. That's why I played dumb.

"Oh, her? No, I don't know who she is . . . er, was. I found her this morning on the beach."

The pirates talked amongst themselves. I figured the twisty guy was translating our conversation for them.

"She is a beautiful American woman," said the twisty guy.

"Yeah, she is."

"She is what?"

"Beautiful. Like you said."

"Not American?"

"I don't know if she's American or not," I said. "I only found her on the beach this morning." That twisty guy was trying to catch me lying. His twisty brain matched his body.

"Did you pull her up from the beach?" he asked.

"Yes, this morning."

"All by yourself?"

"By myself."

The twisty guy's brown eyes scanned me from my sneakers to my mochaccino scalp. "You carried her all by yourself?" he repeated, smiling.

"She was heavy, but yeah, all by myself."

He stared at me, the smile never leaving his smooth face.

"You don't think I'm strong enough?" I asked.

He translated this for his friends. They must

have found this interesting, because they talked and whispered and barked for quite a time.

The big guy relaxed his grip on his rifle. The limping guy leaned against a tree trunk and lit up a cigarette. The twisty guy reached his hand behind his back and rested a hand on his hip. Then he said to me, "Let's see how strong you really are. I have made a bet with my two friends."

"A bet?"

"They do not think you did it. Carried that woman all by yourself. But I say you did. I say that you don't have to look like a horse to be strong." He glanced over at the giant in the black shorts. I wonder if his friend knew he was being called a horse?

"This is our bet," said the twisty guy. "You must carry Kao to the beach."

"Carry a cow?"

"Kao Li Ho." The twisty guy jerked his thumb over at the smoking pirate. The fellow who dropped the coconut on his foot. "You carry him on your back all the way to the beach," said the twisty guy. "Then we believe you."

"I can't do that!"

"Do not make me lose my bet, young American. Show us how strong you are."

I looked at Kao Li Ho, a stupid grin splitting his face. Then I looked at the rifle in the muscleman's hands.

"Okay," I said. "If I do this, do I win anything?"

"Oh, yes," said the twisty man. "You help me win the bet and you will not be shot."

Fair enough. I bent down so Kao Li Ho could jump up on my back. He was about the same size as

Dr. Carpenter, which is probably why they picked him. Thank goodness I didn't have to lift the ox man with the tree-trunk neck.

These pirates in the blue bandannas were weird. First turtle eggs, now this.

I grabbed Kao's sweaty legs on either side of my stomach. He gripped my shoulders, laughing to his friends. *Uff dah!* He felt much heavier than the doctor. My own legs felt wobbly. I was still weak from swimming two nights before, but I was determined to reach the beach.

Slowly I plodded through the forest toward the beach. My shoulders ached all the way down to my tailbone. Luckily, the path was shady. If I had been forced to carry this guy in the broiling, tropical October sun, I don't think I would have made it.

Yuck. Kao's cigarette smoke stank. My eyes watered up, and it was hard to see the path. I didn't want to rub the tears from my eyes because I was holding Kao's legs. No way was I going to touch my face with his sweat on my hands. I blinked about a hundred times. All I could make out were fuzzy green blobs and a vanilla-colored smear glittering behind them.

What seemed like years later, my sneakers finally touched the beach. I felt the hard path give way to soft sand.

Kao jumped down and I fell onto my knees. Ha! I had done it. Sweat rolled down my forehead. With the end of my T-shirt, I wiped my stinging eyes.

The twisty guy was happy. He laughed and jumped around in a odd circular dance step as Kao and the giant handed him what looked like pink, oversize dollar bills from their pockets. I noticed the bills had a picture of an airplane on them.

"Thank you, young American," said the twisty guy. "I did not believe a skinny boy like you could do it."

"Then why did you make the bet?" I said.

"For fun," said the twisty guy.

Some fun.

The pirates exchanged more heated words. The twisty guy nodded to them as if to say, okay, okay. Turning to me, he said, "One more bet."

"Not another one!"

"My friends are still not convinced. Especially Gong."

Gong, huh?

"Gong wants you to lift one more body, then he will be convinced."

"I have to lift *him?*"

The twisty guy laughed. He told his friends and they laughed, too. I was glad everyone was having such a good time.

"No, no, no," said the twisty guy. "Not Gong. You must lift the woman again."

This was going too far.

"Dr. Carpenter is dead," I said. "That would not be respectful."

The twisty guy froze. "What did you call her?"

Oops. "Her? Her who?" I said.

"You called the dead woman by name. But you said that you did not know her."

"No, I don't know who she was. But, um, she

had, you know—"

"What?"

"Uh, papers on her. Identification."

"ID?" asked the twisty guy.

"Yeah, ID."

"Let us go and look at this ID. Then you will have to lift her across the beach. Otherwise Gong will not be happy that I won the first bet so easily."

What should I say? That I found ID and lost it in the water? The pirates would know I was lying. Maybe Dr. Carpenter did have some identification on her, some official card from the *Manta*. If I found anything with writing, I could pretend that it was ID. The twisty guy could speak good English, but he might not be able to read it. Then again, maybe he could. Should I take that chance?

We were walking down the beach toward the grass where Billy and I left the doctor. First Gong, then me, then the twisty guy and the limping Kao. These weird guys were actually going to make me drag a dead body across the sand? It was getting late. Shouldn't they be getting back to their ship?

As we walked I kept glancing into the forest. I thought I might see Billy's face peering out at me from behind a tree, waving a finger at me to keep quiet.

Gong stopped so quickly I almost bumped into him. He spun around and barked something at his buddies. He was so angry he spit. All three of them glared at me.

I stepped around the big-legged giant and stared down at the grass. The imprint of Dr. Jocasta Carpenter's body showed where she had lain that morning.

A new, shallow trench running from the grass toward the water showed us where her body had recently been dragged back to the ocean.

The doctor was out.

7
BLUE JADE

"I didn't touch her!" I said.

All three pirates stared at me.

"I'm telling the truth. I didn't touch her," I said. "How could I have moved her when I was with you guys all the time?"

Once the twisty guy translated for his buddies, this made sense to them.

"Someone else is on this island," said the twisty guy.

"Who?"

"You are not alone."

"No, I mean, yes, I am," I said. "I'm by myself. But, um, I'm sure my friends will come looking for me in their ship."

The pirates strolled up and down alongside the shallow trench, searching for clues. No footprints except ours. I figure whoever dragged poor Dr. Carpenter into the ocean had pulled her feet first, backing into the surf. That way their footprints were covered up by the doctor's body dragging over them. Simple explanation. Occam's Razor.

The clump of seaweed that had covered Dr. Carpenter when I found her was now dry and brown. Besides the missing Joke, the beach looked strangely empty. Something about it worried me.

Boom.

The pirates starting yakking again. "Come with us," said the twisty guy.

They marched me back through the coconut forest, using the same path Billy had raced over when we heard the booms the first time. That noise must be a signal to the pirates. Or a warning.

When we reached the other side of the island, near the sky-blue ship, the beach was deserted. The formerly smooth sand was pockmarked with hundreds of holes. Must have been a good day for eggs.

"Clown turtles, huh?" I said to the twisty guy.

His smooth face grew puzzled. "How do you know about the turtles?"

Oops, again. How would a kid like me know about these creatures? I better not slip up again, or the pirates would learn Billy was on the island. "Well, uh—" I knew a lot of the islands in the Great Barrier Reef had odd names: Magnetic Island, Dunk Island, One Tree Island. "Well," I said. "Isn't this Clown Turtle Island?"

The brown eyes in the twisted face bored into my brain. "Perhaps some people call it that," he replied. "That is not the name we give it. Here, into the boat."

"But my friends—" I cried.

"Forget your friends."

Kao shoved me into a low-lying boat near the shore. Then he, Gong, and their twisted pal piled in, revved up the outboard motor, and aimed us toward the pale blue ship.

The pirate vessel was not a sailing ship, but a powerboat, stretching a hundred feet in the turquoise water. There was a lower deck and an upper deck with a railing wrapped around it. On top of the double-decker pilothouse sat a good-sized satellite dish. The pirates must get great TV. When I clambered up an aluminum ladder and over the side, helped by the poking and prodding Kao behind me, I was greeted by a dozen other curious men. Dark-haired or shaved bald, they looked Asian or Hawaiian, with sharp cheekbones, strong features, and black, intense eyes. A few of them didn't shave, none of them had bathed recently, but each man wore a blue bandanna somewhere on his body like the three buddies who had captured me.

My arrival set off an outburst of voices. A few American words were mixed in with the other rougher, stranger sounds. I was guessing that Gong and Kao were explaining all about the twisty guy's bet. A few of the men looked sternly at me, nodding, sizing me up. Those who shook their heads were treated to a smack by Gong's massive fist. Great! I'll bet they want a demonstration of how I carried Kao to the beach. Couldn't I first have a glass of water?

Thunder echoed across the deck.

I looked up and saw a clear, blue sky. The pirates, however, scattered to each side of the ship, port and starboard. On the upper deck, staring down at us, gripping the rail with two meaty hands the size of bear claws, stood the source of the thunder. Another giant, bigger than Gong. And this giant was a woman.

"Corkscrew!" she shouted to the twisty guy and his friends. "I told you men to bring back eggs." She jerked her massive head toward me. "It looks like this one has already hatched."

Roars of laughter filled the deck.

The giant smiled.

"He is a skinny turtle, but strong," said Corkscrew. Fitting name for that weird, twisty pirate. He stepped to his left and turned his face toward me on his right. One of his hands whipped around from behind him and shoved me closer to the upper deck.

The giant bent her head and inspected me. Long black hair fell like a flag on either side of the giant's coppery face. A blue shirt was knotted at her waist. Uncle Stoppard would have called it *cerulean*. Her giant legs were encased in navy blue pants tucked into blue leather boots that reached her knees. I took a better look at her muscular meat hooks gripping the rail. So many thick rings and bracelets circled her fingers and wrists that her copper skin was barely visible. Blue must be her favorite color. Every ring glittered with a blue stone. Blue gems hung from gold chains looped around the barrel of her neck. Rectangles of blue winked by her ears, behind her thick black hair. When she released the railing and stood up straight, I noticed a blue glint of light (a jewel?) flashing from her navel.

Now I knew why all the pirates wore blue. Gang colors.

The giant thundered in another language to her men. Then she gazed at the pirate called Corkscrew and asked, "What is the turtle's name?"

"My name's Finn," I said.

The pirates gasped.

The giant peered down at me. I felt like a bug

under her boot. "Finn," she said. "A good name for someone who will join the fish."

More laughter from the deck.

She snapped her head up and focused her dark eyes toward another section of the deck. "Speaking of fish," she boomed, "I hear that Ji and Eyebrows have also hooked an interesting catch."

Eyebrows must have been the guy standing at the back of the deck with *no* eyebrows. Not a single hair grew on his shiny, leathery head. He and his toothless buddy (Ji probably means Fang) both smiled and nodded. Then Eyebrows shoved a large, shapeless bundle into the middle of the deck. It was a canvas tarp with something squirming beneath it. A wild animal? Eyebrows whipped off the tarp, and there lay a young guy bound hand and foot. An oily rag was tied across his mouth. Billy Pengo.

"Excellent," said the giant. "He will be useful to us. Take him below."

Billy struggled against his ropes, but it was no use. Gong and three other pirates, who looked as if they could get jobs as wrestlers on TV if they ever decided to give up sailing, lifted up Billy as easily as if he were a sack of laundry, then they ducked their heads through a hatchway and disappeared.

The giant woman bellowed a few more words in a foreign language, then added, "Today was a good day. Tomorrow will be better. Tomorrow we have our biggest job ahead of us. Celebrating tonight will not have a good effect on your performance in the morning. Therefore, we will bed down after dinner. Lights out at twenty-one hundred hours."

Twenty-one hundred hours is nine o'clock at

night. I learned that when reading about port, star-board, bow, and stern.

The pirates must have been a late-night bunch. Hearing their leader's new orders, they mumbled and muttered like fifth graders getting more home-work.

"But first," said the giant, "one more piece of business."

Silence fell over the deck.

"Corkscrew!" she boomed.

The twisty guy wriggled forward. He did not look happy. "Yes, Blue Jade," he said.

"I have one question for you."

Corkscrew's soft brown eyes did not blink.

"How did you find the young turtle?" she asked.

Corkscrew gave me a crooked look. "We heard Kao Li Ho crying for help," he said. "Gong and I went to investigate."

"Away from the turtle beach?"

"Yes."

"On the other side of the island?"

"Yes, Blue Jade."

"What was Kao Li Ho doing on the other side of the island?"

Corkscrew glanced nervously back at his friend.

"Uh—"

"Answer carefully," said Blue Jade.

A struggle was going on in Corkscrew's twisty mind. He did not want to rat on his friend Kao, but he didn't want to lie to Blue Jade, either. Ratting on another pirate was probably not good for your health. Lying to Blue Jade, though, was definitely a dangerous idea. I darted a look at the other pirates. Their grim expressions, their clenched fists and tightened lips, told me that they were aware of Corkscrew's sticky position. Each man was thinking what he would do if he were standing where Corkscrew stood.

"What was Kao doing?" repeated Blue Jade.

"I, uh, do not know for a certainty," said Corkscrew.

"I heard he was looking for something to eat," said Blue Jade.

"That may be. I cannot truthfully say. When Gong and I found the boy, Kao joined us a moment later."

"*Kao!*" bellowed the giant.

The fellow limped forward. He chattered out a few words.

"I do not care what you were doing!" Blue Jade screamed at him. "All I know is that you were not working. You disobeyed. You left the beach. What were your orders? Find eggs, return to the ship. That is all. Nothing more."

Kao was shaking.

Blue Jade yelled something, and the four pirates who had disappeared with the tied-up Billy reappeared in the hatchway. They carried two large plastic coolers. King-size. Blue Jade must have changed her mind and decided to let the pirates celebrate after all. That was some heavy beer; it took two big pirates to lug each cooler.

The coolers were plunked down on the deck two feet apart. Yuck. When the lids were removed, I could see that each cooler was filled to the brim with dark, disgusting water. I hoped they wouldn't ask me to join them in a drink.

Eyebrows and Fang grabbed Kao and dragged him in between the two coolers. I don't think he wanted a drink, either, the way he yelled and fought against them. Kao's head was gripped in the crook of Eyebrows' powerful arm, while Blue Jade blared something foreign to the rest of the crew. All the other pirates whispered and mumbled, gesturing at the two coolers. Oversized pink dollar bills with the airplanes on them were yanked out of pockets and held tightly in fists. Some kind of bet, I'll bet.

Blue Jade glared at the fearful Kao. "Make your choice," she ordered.

All the color drained from Kao's coppery face. Sweat dripped down his forehead. He looked first at one cooler, then the other.

"Choose!" said Blue Jade.

Kao lifted his bare right arm. Taking a deep breath and closing his eyes, he plunged the arm up to his elbow in the dark sludge of the right-hand cooler.

Corkscrew hopped over to my side. "What do you think is in the two tanks?" he whispered to me.

"Acid?"

"Guess again."

"Poison?"

"Ah."

Kao was sticking his arm in poison?

Corkscrew pulled a few pink dollars from his shirt pocket, his sharp eyes focused on the trembling Kao. "One tank is water," said Corkscrew. "Plain old dirty water. But the other tank is quite busy."

"Busy with what?" I asked.

"Blue Jade's little pets."

Kao screamed.

Eyebrows and Ji released Kao as he yanked his wet arm out of the tank. A small brown-spotted creature was attached to him. No, two creatures. Wet, brown-spotted, and glowing with brilliant blue rings.

"Is that an octopus?" I said.

"Blue-ring octopus," said Corkscrew. "One of the most poisonous octopi in the world. And a native of the Great Reef. One bite from those creatures and—"

Kao was having trouble breathing. He sucked in huge, trembling gasps of air. His face was twisted with pain. His eyes were as large as saucers, his skin gray.

"Blue Jade gave him a chance," said Corkscrew, chewing on his lip. "If Kao had chosen the other tank, he would not have been bit."

Some choice. How could he tell when both tanks looked exactly alike?

The pirate crew busily exchanged fistfuls of dollar bills and yammered loudly, while poor Kao fell noisily to the deck of the ship. He stared at his friends, who ignored him while counting their pink bills or checking their watches. Then Kao looked up at the giant on the upper deck. His body shook several times. It was all over. Less than a minute, and Kao Li Ho was dead.

Eyebrows and Fang lifted the lifeless body and tossed it carelessly over the side of the ship. Meanwhile, Blue Jade had climbed down the ladder from her perch. She walked over to the tanks and bent down. Without hesitating, she gently picked up the two octopi who had slipped off of Kao and fallen onto the deck.

"Ah, my little Fluffy and Mittens," she cooed.

Wasn't she afraid of being poisoned?

Blue Jade slipped the slimy creatures back into their cooler. "Good job," she said. "Now run along and join Whiskers and Princess. There you go."

Blue Jade gazed lovingly into the murky water of the octopi's cooler. Then she glanced over at me. "It is good to have pets," she said.

8
PRISONERS IN THE DARK

"Down the steps, boy."

Corkscrew poked my shoulder blades with the business end of his rifle. I carried my backpack in my hands. Once the pirates convinced themselves there was nothing valuable in my stuff, they let me keep it. At gunpoint, Corkscrew forced me down the hatchway, along a dim hallway, down a second, shorter flight of steps, and through another hallway that was darker and smellier than the first. The passageway dead-ended with a choice of three doors. Corkscrew faced the left-hand door, produced a key from a chain round his swivelly neck, and unlocked the middle door without looking at it. I peered cautiously inside the opening. The cold metal of Corkscrew's rifle shoved against my shoulder blades again. The door slammed shut, the lock turned with a click.

"Finn!"

I couldn't believe it. "Uncle Stoppard?"

Before my eyes could adjust to the darkness, an invisible pair of arms wrapped me in a bear hug. "I thought you had drowned," said Uncle Stoppard.

"I thought I did, too," I said. "For a second. But lucky I was wearing my life jacket."

"Where were you? What happened?"

I explained to Uncle Stoppard about swimming to the island that was not Reversal Island. And how I had run into the turtle-egg hunters.

"They made you carry a cow?" said Uncle Stoppard.

"The guy's name is Kao," I said. "Or rather *was* Kao. They killed him. I mean, Blue Jade did. She made him put his arm into a cooler full of poisonous octopi."

"I've had the pleasure of seeing them yesterday," said Uncle Stoppard. "Mitzi and Foofy."

"Mittens and Fluffy," I said.

"Whatever."

"The guy died in seconds. It was horrible."

"One octopus contains enough venom to kill ten adults," said Uncle Stoppard.

"How do you know that?"

"I read a lot."

Yeah, that book called *Danger Below.*

"Where's Captain Stryke?" I asked.

• "They shot him, Finn. Not long after the outburst, Stryke and I saw a blue ship off Reversal Island. Our engine and lights weren't working. I guess the lightning took them out. So Stryke fired a flare. The ship came alongside the *Forty-Niner,* and a pack of guys starting boarding her. Stryke whispered to me that they were pirates, but I had figured that out for myself, noting their machine guns and obvious lack of personal hygiene. Remember that gun Stryke said he carried? Well, he never got the chance to fire it. A pirate shot him twice. A weird, creepy guy all twisted round and round like a—"

"Corkscrew," I said.

"Exactly, like a corkscrew."

"That's his name," I said.

"Charming," said Uncle Stoppard.

"I'm sorry about Captain Stryke, but I'm glad they didn't shoot you," I said.

"They almost did. Then they found out I was an American. These guys think all Americans are rich."

"You *are* rich," I pointed out.

"Temporarily rich," he said. "But at the rate we're spending it, looking for your parents and . . . I'm sorry, Finn. I just meant that—"

"I know what you meant."

"We're still not that far from Reversal Island."

Locked in a closet on a ship crawling with armed pirates, we might as well be on the opposite side of the planet from that stupid island. "Think the pirates will let us go?" I asked.

"I'm working on a plan," said Uncle Stoppard. "Like I said, they think I'm rich." His tone of voice grew angry. "I told them I was a mystery writer, and that convinced them I was dripping with dough."

"Why?"

"Because of that blasted Mona Trafalgar-Squeer, that's why."

Mona Trafalgar-Squeer is the coolest mystery writer on the planet. Next to Uncle Stoppard, of course. Critics call her the Queen of Crime, the Baroness of Bafflement, the Diva of Deception. Her puzzling plots are titanic. You can never figure them out until the last page, sometimes not until the last word. And she gives you all the clues, too. Mona's a British citizen, but she spends half the year in Minneapolis, zipping around the city streets on her silver Kawasaki, or locked in her apartment overlooking the Mississippi River. She and Uncle Stoppard met once—Mona even helped me rescue Uncle Stop from a crazy killer—but for some reason the two of them do not see eye to eye.

"Queen of Crime, ha!" he always says. "It's a crime her books sell."

"I heard a few pirates mention Mona's name before they brought me down here," I said.

"They're *still* talking about her?"

I didn't have the heart to tell Uncle Stoppard that the pirates had discovered one of Mona's paperbacks in my backpack. It's her most recent book. I packed it to read during the long air flight to Australia. I, uh, I've read all of Uncle Stoppard's stuff. Anyway, the pirates saw it and recognized Mona's picture on the back cover. She's famous all over the world; her books have been translated into twenty-six languages. I suppose when pirates aren't looting ships or digging up eggs or making up bizarre bets, they get bored and want something to read.

Eyes Cubed is the name of Mona's paperback. The villain in the book makes a radio transmitter that emits powerful mind-bending vibrations. The vibrations change the shape of people's eyeballs—turning them into cubes—making normal-sighted people nearsighted or farsighted or whatever. When ordinary citizens and cops are unable to see correctly, the villain robs banks and jewelry stores. No one can give an accurate eyewitness description of the crook because no one can see straight. Clever, huh? The detective who eventually tracks down the villain is blind.

"Simply because Mona is filthy rich, the pirates believe that all mystery writers are," said Uncle Stoppard. "Including me. So they're holding me for ransom."

"Ransom? Who are they going to demand money from?"

"I don't know. The government, maybe. My agent. But I think I can exchange my freedom—our freedom—for cash and get the money for them myself."

"There aren't any cash machines on board," I said. "And I doubt these guys will take a check."

"Think they'll take American Express?"

A muffled chuckle came from the corner. Do rats laugh?

"I forgot about him," said Uncle Stoppard. In the dim light I picked out a man's figure in the corner. Billy Pengo, still bound hand and foot. Uncle Stoppard untied the rag from his mouth.

"I thought you had escaped," I asked.

"Shhh," he hissed.

"What's wrong?"

"I don't want those jerks to hear us," he whispered.

"Turn around and we'll untie you," I said.

"No, I don't want to make them any angrier," said Billy. "I gave 'em a good fight before they trussed me up like this."

"You kill anyone?" I asked.

"With my bare fists? Not likely, kid," said Billy. "But I don't want to end up like Carpenter, either."

"Pardon me for interrupting," said Uncle Stoppard. "But how do you two know each other? Finn?"

I explained to Uncle Stoppard about meeting Billy Pengo on the beach. How he had saved my life from the geography cone. And how we had found the dead body of his team member, Dr. Jocasta Carpenter. The purple lips.

"Sounds like asphyxiation," said Uncle Stoppard.

"Looked like it, too," I said. I told Uncle Stoppard how I had carefully examined the doctor's body. He nodded in agreement when he heard my theory about how Dr. Carpenter could not have drowned once she left the *Manta*.

"The pirates must have killed her," Billy hissed to himself.

"Not the pirates I was with," I said.

"Are you one of the scientists?" Uncle Stop asked.

Billy shook his head. "Crew. We were on our way to the southern Barrier Reef at Heron Island when lightning struck our ship last night."

"Lightning struck you, too?" said Uncle Stoppard.

"Weird, huh?" I said. "And remember who sponsored the *Manta*?"

"How could I forget?" said Uncle Stoppard. "The Ackerberg Institute."

"They're not going to be happy about that ship," I said.

"You know the Institute?" asked Billy Pengo.

"Too well," said Uncle Stoppard, grimly. "You sure you don't want us to untie you?"

"Nah, that's cool. Besides, they didn't use rope on me. It's those bloody plastic ties." The white plastic loops that police use during a riot or a drug raid. I've seen them on *Cops* and *Highway Patrol*. "These babies would have to be cut off," said Billy Pengo.

I had a knife in my backpack, hidden in an inside zipper. The pirates missed it. In Billy's corner I noticed a dark shadow on the floor for the first time. "What's that?" I asked.

"Oh, that? My knapsack," said Billy. "I had it when the pirates jumped me. They threw it in here once they checked it for valuables."

"What's that?" rasped Uncle Stoppard.

"His backpack," I said. "Weren't you listening?"

"I mean, out there," said Uncle Stop.

The three of us had been speaking in whispers. I'm sure the pirates couldn't hear us, but we heard heavy footsteps outside in the hall.

"Quick, the gag!" said Billy.

Uncle Stoppard hurriedly shoved the rag between Billy's teeth. The door flew open. It was the mighty Gong. He barked a few words, handed Uncle Stoppard a metal jug, threw something in my lap, and slammed the door.

"Crackers," I said.

Billy spit out the gag. "I'll say he's crackers. The whole lot of 'em are crazy."

"Crackers to eat," I said, holding up the plastic bags that had landed on my lap.

"Here, Finn. Have some water," said Uncle Stoppard.

Water! I had forgotten how thirsty I was. I raised the jug's mouth to my dry lips. Ahhhh.

"Save some for the rest of us, Finn."

We took turns drinking from the jug and munching the stale, dry crackers. Uncle Stop would stick a cracker in Billy's mouth and I'd hold the jug to his lips.

"Crackers ain't so bad," said Billy.

Coconuts would have been better, but who was complaining? Nothing was so delicious in the world as plain, cold water after you'd lugged a pirate on your back and seen two dead bodies in one day.

"Tastes like champagne," said Billy.

"What do you think the pirates want from us?" I said.

"I think we'll find out soon enough," said Uncle Stoppard.

Heavy footsteps approached. This time it was our old friend Corkscrew who opened up the door, the man who had shot Captain Stryke. He rousted me and Uncle Stoppard to follow him. Billy Pengo was kept tied up in the corner. Did Blue Jade and her pirates think he was dangerous? Uncle Stoppard was taller than Billy and just as strong. Maybe the pirates didn't like New Zealanders.

At the moment I didn't care where Corkscrew was leading us. I was glad to get out of that dark and stuffy little room. The twisty man stopped beside a new door.

"Peeeuuh! What died in there?" I said. Maybe that wasn't such a wise thing to say on a pirate ship. Considering I had seen how they treated one of their own shipmates.

"Inside," said Corkscrew.

Uncle Stoppard and I stepped in and were

immediately swallowed up by a foul, colossal stench. Rotten eggs, raw fish, pickle juice, cigarette smoke, mildewed vegetables, curdled milk. Uncle Stoppard pinched his nose. My eyes watered like a squeezed lemon. Well, now we knew what the pirates wanted from us.

Clean the kitchen.

9
A PIECE OF OCTOPI

Galley is the technical term for a ship's kitchen. And technically speaking, this galley stank. Orange stuff with beans in it plastered the walls. Thick black grease coated the top of the stove. Greasy fingerprints were smudged on handles, cabinets, drawers, and the refrigerator. The sink was a fire hazard. Dirty dishes hid the countertops. Heaping bags of rotting food, plastic containers, and fish heads were piled against one wall like an avalanche.

In sixth-grade art class, we learned about this famous painter, dead now, who flicked gobs of paint at his canvas. Then he laid his painting flat on the floor, tugged on his cowboy boots, and stomped all over it. *Voilà*, a masterpiece. It wouldn't have surprised me to find this painter's signature scrawled in a corner of the kitchen. For the splotchy, colorful murals on these walls, however, he threw away his paint and used soy sauce, mustard, ketchup, something thick and brown like barbecue sauce, and a stinky green gunk that Uncle Stoppard called *wasabi*.

That was the good news. The bad news was the

kitchen had become the home for a few hundred cockroaches. No, make that a thousand. Whenever I tugged open a sticky drawer, I saw dozens of the brown buggers skitter over silverware and squeeze through cracks in the wood. White plastic bags full of week-old food were alive with tiny legs, feelers, and wings. Uncle Stop has a friend in South Carolina where the cockroaches live happily year-round in the hot, humid air. His friend told him that for every cockroach you can see, there are fifty more that you don't see. Which means for every square foot of the pirate ship, the roaches outnumbered the humans by a hundred to one. Thinking about them gave me an itchy feeling on my back and arms and legs. Do the coral polyps feel this way about the millions of zoox-anthellae creeping up and down their insides all day long?

Uncle Stoppard and I were handed cruddy plas-tic buckets, rags, and a broom. Nothing else. Several hours later I think we had cleaned off maybe one tabletop and the handle on the refrigerator door. Corkscrew came to fetch us and marched us back to our dark prison cell. He handed us more crackers and water.

"You guys smell like you were swimming in the head," whispered Billy Pengo.

"Worse," I said.

No, I was wrong. Worse came later. This time Gong led Uncle Stoppard and me back to the scene of the crime. Dinner had been served and more plates and garbage awaited us. Stale cigarette smoke hung in the air. I noticed extra eggshells in the sink. Tables were littered with empty beer cans.

While we scrubbed the grimy walls, I asked Uncle Stoppard, "What are clown turtles?"

"The turtles who make the other turtles laugh?" he said.

"I'm serious."

"Never heard of them, Finn. I've heard of clown fish and clown treefrogs, though. The turtles must be a rare delicacy," he said. "The pirates could be running a black market with cooks and chefs throughout the South Pacific. I've read about chefs in fancy Hong Kong restaurants who pay traders up to a thousand dollars for a special bird's nest for soup."

"Who'd want to eat a soggy nest?"

"Europeans think Americans are disgusting for eating peanut butter."

"But peanut butter is normal," I said. "You can buy it at the store."

Why were we talking about food? This whole place destroyed my appetite. The thought of feathers, twigs, and eggshells floating in a bowl of soup made me gag.

After hours of scrubbing a few square yards of wall and soaking all the dirty dishes and bowls and pans—I wished we had rubber gloves—Gong and his trusty rifle hauled us back to our quarters. Billy was asleep, his hands still bound behind him, his head slumped against the wall. I was dead tired. More tired than I was from the night of floating and swimming in the ocean.

"Uncle Stoppard," I whispered. "Are you still working on your plan for giving money to the pirates if they let us go free? Uncle Stoppard? . . . Uncle Stop?"

He was snoring on the dark floor. I leaned against the wall and closed my eyes. Pink shells. For some reason, I was dreaming about gathering pink shells on the beach of Reversal Island with my dad and mom, when a loud noise woke me. Voices rumbled in the hall. Billy and Uncle Stoppard woke up, too. It must have been around midnight. I leaned over and placed my ear against the door. No good, because I couldn't understand what the pirates were saying. Sounded like a dozen of them out there in the crowded hall. Were they placing another crazy bet?

The lock clicked above my head. I stumbled back as the door crashed open. Corkscrew was yelling at the top of his voice. Then he switched to English. "How did you get out of this room? Answer me!"

"What are you talking about?" said Uncle Stoppard.

"We've been in here all night," I said.

"Impossible," he said.

"How could we get out?" I asked. "We don't have a key."

"What's going on?" said Billy Pengo.

Corkscrew and several of his buddies crowded into the room and yanked us to our feet. They dragged us down the hall. Gong was lying on the floor of the hallway. Pirates surrounded him, checking him out, examining his clothing. Gong's lifeless hands no longer held his rifle.

Up on the deck a half-moon and a million stars sailed in a black sky. A few orange lights glowed from the pilothouse windows. Everyone's face was wrapped in shadows. Blue Jade stood once more on the upper deck, gripping the rails with her massive hands and looking down at her subjects. Seconds after we were pushed onto the deck, Gong's body was carried out by the rest of the crew and dumped on the spot where Kao's body had dropped earlier in the day.

Blue Jade did not shout. Her voice was quiet and grave. "Who did this?"

No one answered. Waves slapped against the side of the ship. It was silent enough for me to hear the pirates breathing. All of them except Gong.

Blue Jade repeated, "Who is responsible for this?"

Corkscrew gyrated forward. "We were sleeping, King Bee."

Did he really call her King Bee? What was that all about?

"Not everyone was sleeping," said Blue Jade.

Eyebrows shouted and gestured toward me and Uncle Stoppard. I think he was scowling, but it's hard to tell without eyebrows. Corkscrew said, "None of us wanted to kill Gong. Why should we? He was our friend."

Yeah, a friend like Kao.

"Only the strangers would want to kill him," said Corkscrew. "They were probably planning an escape. Gong saw them and they killed him."

"No," said Uncle Stoppard. "We were in our room the whole time."

"We don't even have weapons," I said.

"Silence!" ordered Blue Jade.

"Gong was found on the floor outside their room," said Corkscrew. "The crew was asleep in their beds, Blue Jade. No one else was in the lower hallway."

"What was Gong doing down there in the first place?" I said.

"Guard duty," said Corkscrew, spinning to face me, sort of. "Gong was checking the hallways. That was his schedule. He heard a noise in your room, opened the door, and you jumped him. It was part of your plan."

"That's not true," said Uncle Stoppard.

"It never happened," I said.

Corkscrew ignored us and continued his theory for Blue Jade. "The Americans killed Gong, then became fearful, like the cowardly dogs they are. They fled back inside their room, pretending they had never escaped."

"But when you opened the closet door," I said, staring at Corkscrew, "was the door locked or unlocked after you found Gong dead?"

Corkscrew hesitated for a second. "Unlocked," he said.

"That's a lie!" I said. "I heard the lock turn. How could we unlock a door from the inside? We don't have a key."

"Yes, how could we get out?" asked Uncle Stoppard.

"You tricked Gong into opening the door," said Blue Jade. "Then you killed one of my men in your foolish attempt to escape."

A pirate spat at us. I think it was the toothless guy, Fang.

Uncle Stoppard gazed up at the pirate queen. Her black hair glistened like oil in the moonlight. I could hear the creak of her blue leather boots as she leaned back and folded her arms.

"Please, you must believe us," said Uncle Stoppard. "We are unarmed. We were locked in that room. Asleep. We did not try to escape, we *couldn't* escape, and we did not kill your, uh, your employee."

Blue Jade kept looking at Uncle Stop, licking her lips, a weird light in her eyes.

"Believe me," said Billy Pengo, speaking for the first time. "If I had killed your mate Gong there, I sure wouldn't be hanging around here. And tell me"—he turned, addressing the crew—"how could I kill badboy Gong there, with my hands behind my back?"

Corkscrew pointed at me and Uncle Stoppard. "The Americans did it," he said.

Blue Jade boomed out an order, and several guys disappeared down the hatchway. I was getting a bad feeling about this, like the bad feeling I had on the shore of the island when I discovered Dr. Jocasta Carpenter's body.

The four pirates reappeared from below. They lugged out the coolers again.

"You can't do this!" I cried.

Blue Jade looked calmly at Uncle Stoppard. "I shall give you a choice," she said. "We will let the Immortal Ones decide."

The lids were removed from the coolers. Two pirates jumped Uncle Stoppard and dragged him between the coolers.

"You stink!" I yelled at Blue Jade.

Uncle Stoppard looked back at me. He struggled with the guys holding him, grunting loudly, banging into the coolers. They pinned his arms against his back and held him in place.

"We cannot fight against our fate," said Blue Jade. "Your choice will reveal your heart. If you are truly innocent, you will be guided to the empty cooler. If you are guilty, which I believe you are, you will feel the bite of the little ones."

Uncle Stoppard looked toward each of the coolers. They looked exactly alike. The dirty brown water was the same. All at once Uncle Stop's face grew strangely calm. Was he praying? He lifted his left arm, the skin exposed all the way up to the sleeve of his green T-shirt. Quickly he plunged it into the left cooler. Pink dollars were exchanged rapidly among the pirate crew. How could they make a stupid bet when Uncle Stoppard might get killed by those blue-ringed monsters?

Seconds passed. There were no sounds except for the waves slapping against the hull. Please let the octopi be in the *other* cooler.

Uncle Stoppard screamed.

"No, no!" I shouted. Eyebrows had a grip on my T-shirt, holding me back.

Uncle Stoppard stumbled forward onto this knees, next to the fallen Gong. His breathing was fast and wheezy. His cucumber-green eyes grew wide.

This could not be happening. Blood was rushing into my face, banging in my ears.

"Let me go!" I yelled.

Uncle Stop reached out his wet arm, weakly. "Finn—" he croaked.

His body fell with a *thunk* against the deck.

10
DEATHSTING

Blue Jade climbed down her ladder and stood, hands on hips, gazing at Uncle Stoppard's lifeless body.

"Why did you kill him!" I shouted at her.

Her voice was calm. "It was his fate," she said. "He killed Gong. The Immortals killed him. Life is in balance again."

"What are you talking about?" I yelled.

"Toss him overboard," said Blue Jade, turning on her heel.

"No!" I broke free of Eyebrows' grasp and ran at the pirates who were lifting Uncle Stoppard off the floor. I grappled with the first guy and tried to yank Uncle Stoppard's arms loose from the pirate's grip. "Leave him alone!" I muttered.

The pirate flung out his heavy arm and hurled me backward onto the deck. I slid along the floor and bumped into Gong's head.

"Uff dah!"

That did not come from me.

The pirate who struck me had released Uncle Stop's arms and shoulders, dropping his spiky red head against the deck.

"Uncle Stoppard!"

"He is alive," said Corkscrew.

"Alive?" echoed Blue Jade.

A few angry pirates returned pink dollars to their friend's greedy fists.

Uncle Stoppard sat up on the deck, meekly rubbing his sore head.

"You are alive!" I said.

"And I was almost in the water," he whispered to me.

Oh. Uncle Stoppard had been hatching another plan, and I blew it. How was I to know? I was just glad that Mittens and Whiskers hadn't sunk their paws into him.

"You are clever," said Blue Jade.

"I am innocent," said Uncle Stoppard, looking up at her. "The Immortals have decided."

"If you are innocent, why try to deceive me?" said Blue Jade.

"I didn't want my friend Corkscrew to lose any money," said Uncle Stoppard. "I noticed that he had bet against me."

"Well done, Stoppard," cheered Billy Pengo. Corkscrew bowed slyly in our direction.

"I still believe you killed my man Gong," said Blue Jade.

"Throw him over anyway," said Eyebrows.

"Let us see if he can pass the test with the sharks," suggested the toothless Fang.

Uncle Stoppard stood up. "How can I convince you that we had nothing to do with his death?"

"Wait!" I cried. "You know that Uncle Stoppard is a mystery writer. A rich mystery writer, right?"

"Like Mona Trafalgar-Squeer," said Blue Jade, nodding.

"Yes, Mona, Mona," mumbled the pirate crew.

"Uncle Stoppard knows all about murder and clues and how to solve a crime. Let him solve Gong's crime. Him and me, I mean. We can find out who the real killer is."

The pirates were murmuring. Blue Jade glanced at her men, then she scoped out the dead giant lying at her feet. The killer was somewhere on that deck, hidden in the shadows.

"You will find the real killer?" asked Blue Jade.

"We'll give you evidence," I said.

"Uh, we'll need some time," said Uncle Stoppard.

"Twenty-four hours," said Blue Jade.

"That's not enough," said Uncle Stop.

"Twenty-four hours," repeated the King Bee. "And during that time, none of my men will kill you. You may examine Gong's body. Talk to me tomorrow." She gracefully climbed up the ladder and disappeared into the pilothouse.

"Back to your room," said Corkscrew.

"But you heard what she said," I began. "We have to examine—"

"Tomorrow," said Corkscrew. "Tonight, you sleep locked up."

"But—"

"It's for our own good," Uncle Stoppard whispered to me. "We don't want the real killer getting at us before we start our investigation, do we?"

Uncle Stoppard, Billy Pengo, and I were hustled back down the steps and hallways to our stuffy little closet. "I will have Gong's body locked up in another room," said Corkscrew before he shut us in.

"As long as it's not the kitchen," I said.

Click.

"Hear that? That was the sound I heard right before the door was opened."

"How did you do it, Stoppard?" asked Billy Pengo.

"Yeah, you sure were lucky," I said.

"Lucky?" said Uncle Stoppard, his eyebrows arching toward his forehead. "Finn, you were the one who saved me."

"Me? What did I do?"

"You told me how to figure out which cooler had the octopi in it. Or octopuses. Actually, octopuses is the preferred —"

"How, Uncle Stoppard, how?"

"You said it yourself, Finn. You shouted it out while I was being dragged over to those deadly coolers. *Used ink,* you said. Right, I thought. An octopus used ink when it was attacked."

"That's not what I said. I was yelling at Blue Jade. I said, *You stink.*"

You stink. Used ink.

"They do sound alike," said Billy.

"Boy, then I really *was* lucky," said Uncle Stoppard. "I thought you were giving me a clue to figure out which cooler had the octopuses in it."

"How did you do it?" I asked.

"I was struggling with those two big apes," said Uncle Stoppard. "I did that on purpose so I could kick both of the coolers. I was hoping no one guessed what I was up to. Kicking the coolers frightened the octopuses. I thought they might get spooked enough to shoot out some of their ink."

"Did they?"

"That's how I passed the test," he said. "I could see that the water in one of the coolers was darker than the other. Blacker. And I could see the ink spreading through the water. No one else would have noticed it unless they were carefully looking for it. Like I was."

Like his life depended on it.

"So you stuck your hand in the other cooler," I said.

"I was 90 percent sure of myself," said Uncle Stop. "It was that other ten percent that could have killed me."

"I'm sorry I gave you away," I said.

"Not your fault. You didn't know. But I thought if those guys tossed me overboard, somehow I could swim to the island and get help."

"Good plan," I said.

"It came to me in a flash while I was faking my death."

"Looked pretty convincing to me," said Billy.

"Gosh," said Uncle Stoppard. "*You stink* and *used ink*. What would I have done without you, Finn?"

"You made a lot of pirates lose their ringgits," said Billy.

"Ringgits?"

"Those are those pink dollar bills they have. Malay money."

"Is that the language they speak, too? Malay?" I asked.

"Yeah. Malay and Chinese are the two languages everyone speaks," said Billy. "Guys on this ship are from all over. China, Indonesia, Malaysia, even India. Piracy is a booming business in Southeast Asia."

Being a crew member of the *Manta* must have helped Billy meets lots of different kinds of people, and hear lots of other languages.

"Did you guys hear Corkscrew call Blue Jade a king bee?"

Billy chuckled. "Corky said *qing bi*," he said. "It's Chinese for 'blue jade.'"

Oh.

Languages are funny. Each country has a different word for the same thing. It would save a lot of time if we all called things by one name.

The next morning Corkscrew let us out of our prison and took me and Uncle Stoppard to a room a few doors away. It was no bigger than our closet. One wall had a pull out bed, like the kind you see in a train. The bed was covered with a huge lumpy sheet. Gong.

"Don't we even get breakfast first?" I asked.

"Be careful where you wander," said Corkscrew, with a tilt of his head. "Some places on this ship are not safe." He closed the door behind us, but did not lock it.

Gong's body looked longer lying down than it had standing up in the island forest. I started at his feet and Uncle Stoppard started at his black wavy hair and blue, puffy face, examining the giant's skin and clothes. No bruises. No blood. No gunshot wounds in his skin or clothes. I had a creepy feeling.

Gong's body reminded me of Dr. Jocasta Carpenter's body on the beach.

I heard a commotion out in the hall. I opened the door slightly and saw Billy Pengo being led away by Corkscrew and a couple of his pals. His back was facing me, and he gripped his backpack with his bound hands.

"Where are you taking me, you bloody—"

"Where do you suppose they're taking him, Uncle Stoppard?" I quietly shut the door.

"Look at this, Finn," he said. I walked over to his side and bent down. On Gong's right arm was a small puncture wound, and the skin was red and swollen. The wound had been hidden under Gong's shirtsleeve. On the sleeve itself was a puncture hole that matched up with the wound. I looked at Uncle Stoppard.

"Octopus bite," he said.

11
CORKSCREW

"Gong's arm isn't wet," I said.

"Nor his shirtsleeve," said Uncle Stoppard.

"No one said anything about seeing an octopus on his body."

"No, they did not."

"How did an octopus—?"

"That is the million-dollar question," said Uncle Stoppard.

Or the million-ringgit question.

If Corkscrew or the other pirates had seen any sign of Fluffy or Mittens near Gong's body, they would have said something to Blue Jade last night. Unless someone else was using the nasty blue-ringed demons for their own secret purposes.

"Gong's too strong. He'd knock you out if you tried sticking his arm into a cooler," I pointed out. "You think someone threw an octopus at him?"

"Like a grenade?" said Uncle Stoppard. "I don't think so. And how would you handle one of those creatures? You'd need heavy-duty gloves."

I remembered Blue Jade picking up her pets

from the deck after Kao died. She slipped them into their cooler without a worry.

"Maybe someone plopped Fluffy onto Gong while he slept," I said.

"Then he would have died in his bed," said Uncle Stoppard. "Not in the hallway. The octopus venom works almost instantly."

"Yeah, I know."

"Did Gong touch the creatures without realizing it?" he asked.

"They have to be kept in water. Salt water, right? Why would Gong have stuck his arms in any kind of water while he was on guard duty?"

"Especially without rolling up his sleeves. The octopus bit through the fabric."

"Would a wet sleeve dry out overnight?" I asked.

"That's a possibility," said Uncle Stoppard.

Gong's death was turning into a real puzzler.

"We need to find out where those coolers are kept," I said.

I also wanted to scan through my copy of *Danger Below* and find out what it had to say about blue-ringed octopi. Check out the facts on venom, how fast it works. The last time I saw my book, it was inside my backpack. That was before my little dip in the ocean.

"Let's take a stroll," said Uncle Stoppard.

We walked upstairs onto the deck. No sign of Billy Pengo around. No sign of those coolers, either. Plenty of pirates, though. A bunch of them stood near the starboard side, wearing scuba gear, checking their air tanks, preparing for or returning from a dive. Uncle Stop kept walking. He climbed up the ladder, Blue Jade's private ladder, right up to the pilothouse.

"Think it's all right to do this?" I asked.

"Don't worry," he replied, grinning. "Blue Jade promised her men wouldn't kill us for at least twenty-four hours."

Yeah, but didn't she say that only eight hours ago?

A fresh morning wind blew across the ship's upper deck, rippling my T-shirt, blowing away all the stink of the kitchen. No cockroaches up here. The white sun burned in a hot blue sky. The sea was turquoise glass.

"Reversal Island is over there," said Uncle Stoppard, pointing. "Wait a minute! It's gone!"

Gone!

Uncle Stoppard shielded his eyes with his hand. "We're on a different side of the coral island," he said. "The ship must have moved during the night."

Blue Jade, *Qing Bi*, appeared out of thin air like a tropical outburst with muscles.

"What are you doing up here?" she demanded. Her bracelets jangled menacingly on her wrists. The gold chains round her neck gleamed like coral snakes.

"We're investigating Gong's death," said Uncle Stoppard. "Like we agreed."

"Where do you keep the octopi?" I asked.

"What?" she said.

"Okay, octopuses."

"Where are the coolers kept?" asked Uncle

Stoppard.

"You are supposed to be finding a killer," said Blue Jade.

Blue Jade was surrounded by killers, her own crew. I'll bet they had killed plenty. Like poor Captain Stryke. But she wasn't concerned with them, she was worried about one specific murderer. Pirates are a bizarre bunch. They have no problem shooting and robbing strangers, but when one of their own is hurt, or when one of their own disobeys their special set of rules, like Kao did—look out.

"We think Gong was bit by one of the octopi," I said.

"The *zhangyu*? Impossible!" she cried, shaking her head. "They are always locked up."

"Where are they locked?" asked Uncle Stop.

"How could Gong be killed by one of my pets?" she asked.

"We found a puncture mark on his arm," I explained. "An octopus bite."

Blue Jade frowned. She was the kind of person who rarely got confused. And when she did get confused, she didn't like it. "Take me to see Gong," she said. "Now."

Down in the small bedroom, Blue Jade peered carefully at the wound on the dead man's arm. "I do not like the look of this," she said. She stood up, her black hair brushing the ceiling. "You think a *zhangyu* made this mark?"

"If you mean an octopus, yes," said Uncle Stoppard.

"Follow me," she ordered.

Inside the hatchway that led out onto the main

deck stood another, narrower door on the port side of the ship. Blue Jade produced a key and unlocked the narrow door. Cooler air rushed against my bare knees.

"The little creatures cannot become over-heated," said the pirate queen.

The two coolers, one with its lid removed, sat against the far wall of the long, narrow room. In the same wall a porthole let in sunlight reflected off the waves outside.

"Only Gong and I have keys to this room," said Blue Jade. "And when Gong died, the keys went to Meimao."

"Who's that?" I asked.

"Eyebrows."

"I come here alone sometimes," she said. "But whenever Gong, now Eyebrows, comes in, he must bring other crew members. No one else comes in here by himself."

So Gong had the only other key to this room when he died. No one would have dared take it from him, he was too big and strong. Could the killer have removed the key from Gong while he slept, and made a copy—no, no. Too complicated. Remember Occam and his razor.

The question is : if Gong was not bitten by an octopus in this room—and if he had been, he would have died here—how did the octopus leave the room? Only two keys, one door, and one skinny porthole. No other entrances or exits. The door was solid wood with a metal handle like the handle on a refrigerator. A rubber molding went all the way round the door, keeping in the cooler air. Where did the air come from? I noticed a small vent near the ceiling. The vent was grilled and too small for anything to crawl through.

The porthole, however, was large enough to slip an octopus through. But someone would still have to enter the room to remove the octopuses from their coolers.

"Where do you sleep?" I said.

"Excuse me?" said Blue Jade.

"Your quarters," I said. "Where are they?"

"I sleep up in the wheelhouse," she replied.

"I was wondering if someone could steal your key while you sleep," I said.

Blue Jade shook her head violently. "Impossible. The key is here, around my neck," she said. "No one else sleeps in the wheelhouse. The men have orders not to disturb me at night."

Or else they get a little taste of Mittens and Fluffy, I'll bet.

"We need more time to solve Gong's murder," said Uncle Stoppard.

"You believe he was killed?" asked Blue Jade quietly.

"The condition of his eyes and lips point to poisoning," said Uncle Stoppard.

"Last night I saw that he had no marks on his body," said Blue Jade. "I almost believe that he died from a heart attack."

"If it had been a heart attack, his skin would appear more gray," said Uncle Stoppard.

Gong's face was a distinct purple.

"Did you notice any odor, Finn?" he asked.

"Uh, yeah, it was weird. Cinnamon."

"Good nose, Finn. Another sign that he was poisoned and his lungs stopped working."

"Poison. There is no other poison on this ship," said Blue Jade. She looked confused again. The giant stamped her foot and glanced at her watch. "You have until midnight tonight to find his killer," she said.

"That's not enough—"

"Out!" she said.

She slammed the door behind us.

"What is she doing in there?" I asked.

"Who knows? Spending some quality time with Mindy and Fifi."

"Mittens and Fluffy."

"Whatever."

"You think she did it?" I asked.

"Blue Jade?"

"Yeah, think she killed one of her own men and is trying to fake us out?"

"When Blue Jade wants to kill a man she does it in public. There's no reason for her to hide it. Who would she hide it from? You think if her crew learned she had killed Gong that they would argue with her?"

"Probably not."

"None of these pirates appear to be subtle."

"Subtle?"

"Delicate. No that's not the right word. Um, none of these guys seems to hide their feelings. They say what they mean, and do what they say."

"So why would they kill a guy in private?"

"Exactly," said Uncle Stoppard. "I'd expect that if any of the crew killed Gong, they would boast about it. Say they were stronger than Gong."

"They wouldn't boast about it to Blue Jade," I said.

"No, but they'd brag to their buddies."

"Let's go find Corkscrew," I said.

The twisty pirate was sitting on deck, next to the starboard gunwale. That's the nautical term for the side of the ship's hull. The scuba guys were still there. Or were those new divers? Seemed like lots of activity in the water this morning. Corkscrew sat blowing smoke rings over the starboard side, while his feet were aimed toward the port side. The smoke rings were twisty figure eights.

"You paid the *zhangyu* a visit," he said.

"Gong was poisoned," I said. "And we think it was one of those blue-ringed guys."

"Poisoned? How interesting. Where would someone get poison on this ship?" Were those beads of sweat on his forehead?

"Those sucker-guys carry tons of venom, right, Uncle Stoppard?"

"Uh, right."

I needed to check out my *Danger Below* book. I kept forgetting about that.

"Mr. Corkscrew, do you mind if we ask you some questions?" said Uncle Stoppard.

"What manner of questions?"

"About your buddies," I said.

"Have you heard any rumors about Gong's death?" asked Uncle Stoppard.

Corkscrew flicked his cigarette over the gunwale, slung his rifle over his shoulder, and spiraled toward the hatchway. "Let us speak inside," he said.

We returned to the dim lower hallway, our closet door at the other end. Corkscrew was more nervous than I'd ever seen him. He almost tripped coming down the stairs.

"No one on board would want to kill Gong," whispered Corkscrew.

"Did someone lose a bet to Gong?" I asked. "Lose a lot of dough? That makes people mad enough to kill."

Gong wiped his forehead. "Gong was famous for losing bets," he said. "The unfortunate fellow never picked a winner." Including me, I remembered. Gong lost a bundle of pink dollar bills when I carried Kao on my back.

"Have you heard of anyone fooling around with the—uh, *zhangyu*?" asked Uncle Stop.

"Never. No one would dare to touch *Qing Bi*'s pets."

I got it! Ships have medical supplies on board for emergencies. Certain medicines given to the wrong person could kill them. Poison them. Maybe someone used a big hypodermic needle on Gong.

"Is there medicine on the ship?" I asked.

"Yes . . . medicine," said Corkscrew. He fell to the floor of the hallway. "Medicine . . ."

Corkscrew grabbed at my knees, then his sweaty hands slipped away. His smooth face was as blue as the ocean out past the coral reef.

"Uncle Stoppard!" I cried.

The twisty legs gave a final shudder, tying themselves into a knot. The pirate's soft brown eyes stared wide, his purplish lips hung open, his chest stopped heaving for breath. A spooky silence filled the hallway. There it was again. The scent of cinnamon hanging in the dim, humid air.

12
DEAD AGAIN

"Grab his legs, Finn!"

"But—"

"Not his butt, his legs."

"If we move him, and the pirates find out, they'll think we killed him, too."

"He's not dead, Finn."

I grabbed Corkscrew's legs.

"Let's put him in the same room with Gong," I said.

We laid the blue Corkscrew on top of the dead giant, a dirty white sheet between them. There was no other room.

"You think he's alive?" I said.

"He has a faint pulse," said Uncle Stoppard. "I think he's in a coma."

"But how?"

"Poison again, Finn."

"The octopi were locked up," I said. "We saw them in the room with Blue Jade."

"We didn't actually see them," Uncle Stoppard said. "But I believe they were in there. Let's look for a puncture mark on Corkscrew."

The red, puffy wound was on his back, a few inches from the base of his spiraling backbone. A small hole in his shirt matched up with the wound. Like the one Gong had.

"Can an octopus bite through clothes?" I asked.

"Seems so," said Uncle Stoppard.

Danger Below. "I'll be right back," I said.

I stepped into the hallway, making sure no one saw me, then trotted over to our prison cell. Oops, I didn't have a key. I looked closely at the door and realized I didn't need one. The lock was a dead bolt that turned with a switch. If I hadn't always been rushed in and out of the closet, I would have realized it sooner. The clicks I heard didn't come from a key turning in a lock, but the bolt flipping in or out. We still couldn't have unlocked the closet door from the inside.

Billy Pengo was gone! That's right, I had seen Corkscrew hustling him down the corridor earlier. Where was he now? I'd worry about that later. I found my backpack wedged behind the door, snatched it up, and ran back to tell Uncle Stoppard.

"Is he still alive?" I asked.

"Barely, Finn. We need to get him to a doctor."

"Remember this?" I said, holding out the book.

Uncle Stoppard squinted at the cover. "Something *Ice*?" he said.

Wrong paperback. Really wrong. I stuffed Mona's mystery back in the pack.

"Different book," I said.

"It looked familiar," said Uncle Stoppard.

"Did it?" I asked. "Ah, here it is. *Danger Below.*"

The pages were puffy and crinkled from spending a night in seawater, but the print was still good. I turned to a section called "Deadly Australians." Cool pictures. Moray eels, cone shells, jellyfish.

"This is it. Blue-ringed octopus," I said.

Blue-Ringed Octopus.
Scientific name: *Hapalochlaena maculosa* or *Octopus maculosa.*

Those long names, again. Like the zooxanthellae. I guess it was better than "Fluffy."

This pretty cephalopod is the world's only poisonous octopus. It lives in warm, shallow reefs off the coast of Indonesia, Australia, and the Philippines. During the day, the octopus hides among the coral or under rocks. It grabs its prey, invertebrates or wounded fish, and delivers a deadly bite with its strong beak. A single octopus contains enough poison in its saliva to paralyze and kill ten adult humans.

The poison, known as maculotoxin, affects the nervous system. Within five to ten minutes, or sooner, the blue-ring's prey will suffer paralysis, respiratory failure, unconsciousness, and even death. Several humans each year are killed by the deadly creatures. Sometimes the victim doesn't even know that he or she has been bitten. Scientists have reported that close contact with the creatures may also lead to envenomation.

"Envenomation?"

"Poisoning," said Uncle Stoppard.

Maculotoxin may pass directly through a person's skin. Dizziness or rapid-heart rate can occur by merely placing a hand in an aquarium where the octopus has been kept for a long period.

What To Do: If a person has been bitten by one of these creatures, look for a small bite mark and a telltale drop of blood. There is little or no discoloration. Pressure should be placed at the point of entry. Immediate medical attention is required.

Maybe Gong and Corkscrew were injected with water from the octopi's tank. I was right about the medical supplies, after all. Hypodermic needles. Since it was too dangerous, not to mention impossible, to move the octopuses from their locked apartment, the water from the tanks was easier to get at. And the water could have been injected into the pirates by a needle. The coolers themselves had been brought out onto the main deck several times since I had boarded the pirate ship. Anyone could have scooped up some water in a container without being noticed. Especially if everyone else's attention was focused somewhere else: on Kao's body, or Uncle Stoppard.

I tried to re-create a mental picture of the coolers. Who had been standing next to them on the deck?

"We need to get him to a doctor," said Uncle Stoppard.

I opened the door and backed out. "Okay," I said. "I'll tell Blue Jade. Maybe she can get a doctor before any of the other pirates find out."

"Find out what?"

Eyebrows, a rifle over his back, a sinister-looking sword stuck in his belt, stood directly behind me. He and a few other pirates were hauling Billy Pengo down the hall and back into the closet.

"Uh, nothing," I said.

Eyebrows shouldered past me and froze in his tracks.

"You killed him," said Eyebrows.

"Wait," said Uncle Stoppard. "Blue Jade said you can't shoot us until midnight."

"Until *after* midnight," I added.

Pirates don't like to waste a lot of time with conversation. We were hauled back out to the deck, Blue Jade assumed her usual position at the rail, Eyebrows and his shipmates stood in an angry knot behind us.

"He needs a doctor," I said.

"They killed him," snarled Eyebrows. "I saw them go below with Corkscrew."

"We were talking with him," said Uncle Stoppard.

"We didn't kill him—he's not dead," I said. "He's still breathing."

"No, he is not," said Fang, straightening up as he

emerged from the hatchway. "Corkscrew is dead."

Eyebrows struck Uncle Stoppard's head with the butt of his rifle. He sagged to his knees.

"*Qing Bi*, stop him!" I cried.

She must have been startled that I knew her Chinese name. Blue Jade held up a hand. Sunlight glittered off a thousand rings and bracelets. "The twenty-four hours are up," she said. "You were supposed to find a killer. Instead, you give me another dead man."

"Time isn't up yet," I said. Blood was trickling down Uncle Stoppard's neck.

"Corkscrew was a valuable worker," said Blue Jade.

"He was poisoned," I said. "Like Gong."

"Poisoned?" exclaimed Eyebrows. The other pirates muttered and cursed behind me.

"Have a doctor look at Corkscrew's body," I said. "A doctor will prove he was poisoned."

"Corkscrew is beyond a doctor's help," said Blue Jade. "As you and your *jiujiu* are also beyond help."

Were they going to shoot us or haul out the coolers?

"However," said Blue Jade—and I think her eyes were staring at me—"you can help us if you choose. Or the *zhangyu* will choose for you."

"You want me to help you?" I said.

"I can use a skinny turtle like you," she said.

"What for?"

"A treasure hunt," she replied.

They want me to dig up more clown eggs? "I'll help you if you won't hurt Uncle Stoppard," I said.

"Blue Jade does not make deals," said the pirate queen.

"Well, Finnegan Zwake does not help mean, nasty people," I said.

The pirates gasped again.

"You are not in a position to demand anything, young dog," said Blue Jade. "However, I shall not hurt you or the rich mystery writer."

Uncle Stoppard's face was pale. Eyebrows' rifle butt must have whacked him hard.

"Eyebrows!" boomed Blue Jade. "Take the *jiujiu* back to his quarters. Have the boy fitted up for the dive."

Dive? As in underwater?

Last night on the deck, when I got my first close-up look at Blue Jade and her terrorist crew, she had mentioned something about today being a busy day. "Tomorrow we have our biggest job ahead of us," she had said. That's why she nixed any celebrating and sent the crew to bed early. The busy day had something to do with those scuba divers I saw earlier.

Uncle Stoppard was dragged into the hatchway, leaving a trail of bloody drops, while I was spun around and shoved toward the gunwale. A pirate with a black, braided beard held a rubber diving suit up to me, shook his head, then threw it down on a pile. The pile grew larger. None of the rubber suits was small enough to fit me.

"He doesn't need a suit," said Eyebrows. "Just fit him with a tank."

The pirate holding the rubber-suit asked me something in Chinese. He wagged his braided beard inches from my face. I shook my head.

Eyebrows translated for me. "Have you ever dived before?" he asked.

"Yeah, plenty of times," I lied. If I didn't help these guys, Uncle Stoppard was in danger. I knew how to swim and had watched *Jaws* thirteen times. I knew what to do. Breathe normal, don't dive or ascend too quickly, keep track of your time underwater. Should be a snap.

"What are you diving for?" I asked.

"Zhenzhu," said Eyebrows. "Pearls."

"Cool," I said.

"These waters have the largest clams in the world. Elephant clams. They make the world's largest pearls," said Eyebrows. "As big as a man's head. But the clams can swallow up a diver if he is not careful."

Not so cool.

"Why does Blue Jade need me to get pearls for her?" I asked.

"That is what we are diving for. Not what *you* are diving for," said Eyebrows, pointing a grimy finger at my chest.

The other pirate handed me flippers and underwater goggles, then began strapping a heavy air tank on my back. "Then why am I diving?" I said.

"There is new treasure on the reef," replied Eyebrows. "A ship sank a few days ago into the coral, but there is only one way to get inside. A small porthole. Big enough for a skinny American boy."

They wanted me to break into the *Manta* and hunt for valuables.

"I say it is too small," said a pirate, standing in a group a few feet away.

"I say the boy will get stuck," said another.

Money exchanged hands as the pirates glanced at me, giving me the once-over. A few guys even pinched my arms and waist, sizing me up for the porthole down there.

"The boy will get stuck and drown," said Fang.

"The boy will get stuck and then they will bite," said another. More money changed hands.

Bite?

"Greedy parrots!" boomed Blue Jade. She had reappeared at my side. "I hope you are not betting against my diver," she said to her men. "That would make me very unhappy."

The pirates quickly stuffed pink ringgits into their shorts and shirt pockets, mumbling and wandering away from their boss to various sections of the ship.

"This is what you are diving for," said Blue Jade, handing me a sheet of paper. A crudely drawn diagram of the *Manta* showed a path from the porthole to the pilot room.

"Memorize this," said Blue Jade. "Paper will do you no good underwater."

The pilot room, then, was my goal.

"You come back with two objects," said Blue Jade. "A book and a box. They are marked on the paper."

"Two," I repeated.

"If you come back with only one, do not come back at all."

"It will be easy," said Eyebrows. "Smooth as silk." He glanced over my head at the pirate handling the scuba gear and laughed. They both laughed like hyenas.

"The porthole is big enough for me?" I asked.

"The porthole is big enough for you," said Eyebrows. "Also, big enough for moray eels."

13
EELS

Moments later Eyebrows gripped me by the shoulders and set me on the gunwale, my feet dangling in their fins above the green water. "Remember what you are to bring back?" he asked.

"Yeah," I said, nodding. Though it seemed like a weird order.

"Can't I go back to get my book?" I asked. My waterlogged copy of *Danger Below* was sitting in the gloomy room that was now a funeral parlor for Gong and Corkscrew. I wanted to read the section on moray eels.

Eyebrows jerked his head over his shoulder at another pirate behind him on the deck. "This is Yelo," he said. "Do not fool with him."

The pirate was only five feet tall, but had enough muscles in his arms for two pirates. Long black hair fell to his beefy shoulders, and I saw a tattoo of a blue shark ripple across his back as he bent down to pick up his air tank.

"Yellow?" I said. "Like a banana?"

"Yelo is a Tagalog name," said Eyebrows. "It

means ice and snow. He is a cold one. Do not mess with him."

I wanted to tell Eyebrows that in Minnesota you don't mess around with yellow snow, either. Something made me choke back the comment. Maybe it was the deadly looking speargun Yelo was strapping to his right arm.

"Can't I go look at my book, please?"

Eyebrows held me out over the water. "Shut up and put in your mouthpiece!"

He dropped me like a coconut.

Coconuts float. I, on the other hand, plummeted beneath the turquoise waves, fumbling for my air hose. A huge splash told me Yelo had plunged in after me. He swam to my side, turned me around, and the two of us were off.

Boy, was it busy down there! A silver stingray— a flying saucer with eyes and a tail—glided inches above my head. Blue starfish gripped the reef wall a few feet from my flippers, while a jungle of bloodred flowers waved wormy fingers of pink and green in the warm, salty currents. Fish were spotted, striped, beaked, and horned. I counted seven different shades of orange on one streamlined creature that looked like a grinning submarine. Living scoops of lime sherbet wiggled their tiny fins. A rainbow had broken and dropped a thousand pieces into the sea, and each piece became a fish. How did all these darting, swooping, diving creatures keep from bumping into one another all the time?

Why was I diving through all of them?

Not for pearls, said Eyebrows. And not for a book and a box.

My real reason for diving was to protect Uncle Stoppard. And to please Blue Jade, to get on her good side; so that, in turn, she might set us free. So that Uncle Stop and I could reach Reversal Island and finally reunite with my parents.

I'd swim all the way to Reversal Island right now if I could. The air tank would keep me underwater, out of sight from the pirate crew. But I didn't have Uncle Stoppard with me. Instead, I had one of the pirate guys swimming alongside as my personal escort, watching me carefully through his green goggles, a speargun strapped on his arm. The gurgle of bubbles from our two air hoses was the only sound in that vast blue universe.

The wreck of the *Manta* lay thirty feet below our paddling hands and feet. It was the most unusual boat I'd ever seen. While other ships have smooth, rounded hulls, the *Manta* did not have a single curving line. The smooth and seamless midnight-black hull was all angles and sharp edges.

Now I understood why Blue Jade wanted me to help her.

The *Manta* had sunk into a large section of the orange reef. Sharp coral arms, thick as oak trunks, hedged the black ship on all sides. The pirates couldn't enter the ship from its deck, because the *Manta* had sunk sideways. All hatchway doors were blocked by the sharp coral. A few portholes on the ship's starboard side, the side now facing up toward the surface of the ocean, glinted like round mirrors among the poisonous flaming-orange trunks. Deep within the reef, the *Manta* was trapped in its own coral coffin.

The only way inside that coffin was a single porthole. And none of the pirates were small enough to squeeze through one.

As we approached the silent *Manta*, Yelo grabbed my belt and led me to the underside of the black hull. He pointed to a shadowy cave formed by the coral arms. A porthole was in there? Yelo detached a flashlight from his scuba gear and thrust it in my hand. He pointed again and patted me on the back.

Wonderful. This was reminding me way too much of a certain scene in *Jaws*, a scene where the audience screams and jumps out of their seats. I snapped on the flashlight and cautiously approached the coral cave. The light beam was weak. It picked out the porthole deep within the orange coral arms, but nothing on the other side of the round glass. For instance, a detached head à la Spielberg, or the beady eyes of a hungry moray eel.

The porthole glass was thick. I turned back to Yelo and gave a helpless shrug. How was I supposed to break through that? The pirate was the resourceful type. He pulled out a pistol from behind him, steadied his free hand against a coral trunk, and pulled the trigger.

Froooom!

I didn't think guns could work underwater, but evidently this one did. The porthole shattered like a broken mirror. I used the end of the flashlight to scrape away remaining glass chunks. The hole itself was slightly smaller than a basketball hoop. I could squeeze through, but not with my air tank strapped to my back.

I wriggled my shoulders and arms out of the straps that held the tank. Then I held the tank with one arm, pushing it ahead of me into the porthole. I followed closely afterward. I didn't want the air hose to get taut and yank the mouthpiece, or my teeth, out of my face. The hole was tight. I felt Yelo's hands give a helpful shove against the soles of my flippers. Another push and I was inside the *Manta*.

So far, so good, no moray eels.

The flashlight beam played around the inside of a small sleeping cabin. The bunk was vertical, the door at my feet. I swam down through the doorway and into a long hallway lined with more doors, reminding me of the pirate ship floating thirty feet above me. The dark passage was spooky. Red neon fish flitted in and out of my light beam, then hurtled past my ears. A few of the doors hung silently open, moving in slow motion as I swam by. Below, on the wall which was now the floor of the passage, my light rested on a single, unoccupied sneaker. It's weird how something so normal, like a shoe, can give you the creeps when you see it alone in the dark. The dark down here was not empty, either. It was alive with lidless eyes and fins and teeth. I couldn't spot the sneaker's companion. Did a bare foot or leg float somewhere nearby? I expected to see the sleek shadow of a tiger shark turning the far corner of the hallway.

I gained the end of the hallway without meeting any man- or boy-eaters. Seeing Blue Jade's map in my head, I made my way through the dead ship toward the pilot room.

It wasn't hard to find. The door was marked

PILOT ROOM. But in the entryway, several feet from the door, lay the one thing I was hoping not to see. Twelve feet of yellow, mucus-covered skin stretched in a sleepy coil, floating inches above the floor. Or above the wall, I mean. The coil ended in a blunt head, with two fierce black eyes, and an open mouth ridged with dozens of flesh-tearing, snaggly teeth. The moray did not move. I was frozen to the spot. Well, as frozen as you can be when you're floating underwater.

I slowly shrugged myself back into the air-hose straps. I wanted both hands free, just in case. What could two hands possibly do against the chomping jaws of a moray?

Lose a few fingers.

The thick coil of the moray's body moved slightly in the current. The beady eyes faced away from me. Its terrible mouth remained open. Could it be asleep? Uncle Stoppard sometimes fell asleep with his mouth open watching a late movie on TV. Maybe the creature slept the same way.

I wish Yelo had given me some sort of weapon.

A loud bang reverberated through the ship. No! It must be Yelo, trying to get my attention, signaling me to hurry up. If the moray eel was asleep, Yelo's pounding against the hull would surely wake it up.

I cautiously swam over the eel and gripped the pilot room door. Good. The eel's face still pointed in the opposite direction. I made one swift tug and yanked the door open. A man's head floated into view.

This head was attached to a complete body. His eyes were glazed and unblinking, his mouth a small dark cavern. A dark round blotch stained the front of his rippling shirt.

On one hand he wore a thick underwater watch. The high-tech digital display kept counting out the seconds. The compass indicated the body was gliding in a north by northwest direction. Opening the door, I had created a sucking current which pulled the body through the doorway and into the room outside. The room with the eel. The eel revolved slowly. Slowly the man's body drifted into the further darkness. A floater.

Bang! Yelo again.

The moray's eyes blinked. The head twitched. A shudder ran the length of the serpentine, mustard-yellow body.

I pulled the pilot room door shut.

The room was lined with thick, rectangular windows. Each window looked out on a forest of red and purple coral trunks.

Bang!

Yes, yes, I was hurrying.

My flashlight found the cabinet indicated on the map. Inside were thick folders and manuals. I pulled them all out, tossing them over my shoulders, letting them float in the dark water behind me like square, hardcover jellyfish.

Here it was. *Manta Technical Specifications.* Boring title. What would the pirates want with this? They were usually after loot and gold. Turtle eggs weren't exactly gold, but according to Uncle Stop, the pirates could sell them for gobs of money. What would Blue Jade and her crew do with a technical manual?

I stuffed the manual under my T-shirt. Now for

the box.

Blue Jade said it would be in the room, but she wasn't sure where. I checked the remaining cabinets, but no luck. Then I trained the flashlight on the control panels and the corners of the room. There it was, lying in an angle of the wall. A black metal box closed with a simple lock. The box was no bigger than a loaf of bread. Was this one of those famous "black boxes"? That was it. Blue Jade wanted the recording of the disaster. When the Ackerberg officials wanted to retrieve the box for themselves, Blue Jade could sell it to them for a tidy fortune. Blue Jade was the only person I knew who could stand up to the Institute's men in black.

Now, how did I get out of here? I spied a second doorway. I hoped no new morays lay sleeping on the other side.

Wrong. As I opened the door, I saw two of the gross, yellow creatures. They were curled up in a corner of the hallway, their heads facing me like twin gargoyles.

Slowly I swam past, making as little motion with my feet as possible. Four moray eyes turned with me, watching me. Watching the light from my beam slide over the hallway walls and floor.

Perhaps the moray was the kind of creature that did not attack you unless provoked. Unlike pirates.

Bang!

I glided through the black passageways and returned to the original porthole. Yelo's face was peering in. He didn't see me yet, as I shrugged out of the air-tank straps a second time. I easily lifted the tank. Wait. An escape plan hatched itself inside my head. I wondered if this was how Uncle Stoppard felt when he pretended to die from the octopus bite?

The air tank. I could leave it inside the ship, close to the porthole. Uncle Stoppard and I could swim down here, get the tank, and use it to swim underwater to Reversal Island. The pirates wouldn't see us on the surface. They would have to follow underwater. But if Uncle Stoppard and I could steal a second tank . . . I saw lots of tanks being used up on the pirate ship.

Bang!

Uncle Stoppard and I could swim underwater at night. I snapped my flashlight into an oversize pocket on my cargo shorts. Maybe Yelo would forget about it if he didn't see it.

The problem was, how to get away with not bringing my tank with me. What kind of excuse could I give to Yelo and Eyebrows? I didn't want that speargun aimed at me.

I handed Yelo the manual and the box. That would give him something to think about. Then I climbed back out the porthole backward, dragging my air tank behind me. As soon as I cleared the porthole, except for the hand holding the tank strap, I froze my body. I was going to take one last, huge gulp of air from my mouthpiece, but the hose caught on something. I let go of the tank, just inside the porthole. Better hurry, I thought. I widened my eyes. I grabbed Yelo and tried to look as terrified as I could. I acted like a nutcase. I chomped my teeth and pointed back toward the porthole.

Moray eel, I tried to signal him.

He got it. Yelo glanced over my shoulder at the open porthole, then took off. Not only did he forget about the air tank, he forgot about me. I swam after him, rushing upward toward the bottom of the ship's hull, holding my breath.

My lungs were on fire.

How long did it take to rise up thirty feet of water? I remembered from *Jaws* that if a diver ascended too quickly, he could get deathly sick, get something called "the bends." Your lungs would give out on you.

I didn't care. I needed air.

The ship's shadow seemed to retreat farther and farther away. Little black dots swam before my eyes, the sides of my head started to pound like jackhammers.

My nose fought to breathe. No, I can't even take in a little water. One tiny gulp and it was all over, the floodgates would pour in. My lungs pushed against my rib cage. The pressure to breathe was almost unbearable. I pushed with all my strength and paddled fiercely with my swimming fins. I clawed at the water, climbing upward and upward.

My arms felt limp as rubberbands.

Then my head crashed through the surface. Sunlight burned in my eyes, and my mouth burst open. I thought my lungs would never stop burning. Weird, I exhaled first, like a popped balloon. Then I gulped for air. There wasn't enough oxygen in the whole world to satisfy me.

Somehow I ended up on the deck of the ship. I lay on my side and sobbed for more oxygen, my rib cage aching as if I had been punched in the gut. The pirates were busy looking at the manual, ignoring my half-dead body.

"This book'll make more money than Mona Trafalgar-Squeer's ever did."

"You lost your bet, Eyebrows," said Yelo. "The boy found the box, after all."

That creep bet against me?

My brain was spinning with visions of moray eels and floating dead bodies. Some escape plan. A priceless air tank now lay below the pirate ship, an air tank that only the skinny American boy could get at. But unless Uncle Stoppard and I had a second tank to use, how could I ever find my way down to that coral coffin before my lungs ran out of air?

14
BLUE POISON

I smelled cinnamon.

"Uncle Stoppard?"

"I'm here, Finn."

"This isn't the closet."

"No, this is the room where we kept Gong and Corkscrew," said Uncle Stoppard.

"But where are—?"

"Consigned to a watery grave," said Uncle Stoppard. "Like their friend Kao Li Ho."

Holy cow! "You mean their bodies were dumped overboard?"

Uncle Stoppard nodded grimly. "After you went on your diving expedition, they came and took away the bodies. I heard both splashes."

I sat up from the sleeping room bunk. The room grew dark and dizzy.

"Careful," said Uncle Stoppard. The bruises where he had knocked his head on the *Forty-Niner* hatchway glowed an ugly yellow. "You could have gotten seriously hurt down there."

I dropped back onto the bunk. "Uff, what a headache!"

"Never hold your breath when you come up, Finn. That's why you feel terrible. You had plenty of oxygen in your lungs. Exhale when you ascend. Otherwise your lungs could burst."

"Did that Yelo guy tell you what happened?" I asked.

"You lost your air tank and were attacked by a moray eel. You were lucky they didn't bite you, Finn. The pirates were telling me about a guy bit by an eel, and they had to saw the eel's head off because he wouldn't let go. Why are you laughing?"

"That's not a laugh, it's more of a chuckle."

"It's more of a wheeze. You sound terrible."

I explained my escape plan to Uncle Stoppard.

"Sounds like you were suffering from a lack of oxygen *before* the attack," he said.

"I was not attacked," I said. "That was all fake. But there were moray eels in the ship. Three of them."

"Gross."

"Why don't you like my escape plan?" I asked.

"How do we get down there, Finn? We need a second tank to get down to the first one."

"We steal it."

"Steal?"

"Okay, we borrow it."

"From pirates?"

"We can't make the pirates dislike us any more than they do already."

"You have a point. But Blue Jade might let us go, now that you found the treasure she was looking for."

"Some treasure," I said. "A book and the black

box." I explained about the technical manual. "By the way, where is Billy Pengo?"

"I haven't seen him, Finn. I wonder if the poor guy didn't end up with Gong and Corkscrew."

I had a theory about that.

"Uncle Stoppard, I have a theory about that."

"About—?"

"About Billy Pengo. Remember when I saw him being taken out of our cell by Corkscrew, when we were examining Gong's body? Where did they take him? That's the first thing to think about. Then, today, when Blue Jade showed me a map for reaching the pilot room of the *Manta*—how did she know where it was?"

"Good question."

"I don't mean just the book. I mean the ship, too. The *Manta* was hit by lightning and sank days ago. The same evening the *Forty-Niner* was struck. But the pirate ship was on the other side of the island. They didn't see the *Manta* sink. They probably didn't even know about it. According to Billy Pengo, the scientists were taking an alternative route down to the Barrier Reef. No one would know the *Manta* was in these waters, except for the people who were on the *Manta*."

"Pengo," said Uncle Stoppard.

"Bingo," I said. "And how would Blue Jade know where the technical manual was kept?"

"Pengo must have told her," said Uncle Stoppard.

"To save his skin. He made a bargain with Blue Jade, like you were thinking of doing. Only he gave them the *Manta*. He's probably having dinner with Blue Jade right now. Waiting for the pirates to put him ashore at the next safe port."

"You can't blame him for that, Finn. Yes, I know, the ship was not his to give away. But if I were in his shoes, I might do the same thing."

"It's not loyal," I said.

"Who was he hurting?" asked Uncle Stoppard. "Everyone on the ship seems to have been killed or disappeared."

Yeah. Everyone on the ship. Talk about a bizarre coincidence.

There was a second bizarre coincidence. All three pirates who had found me on the island—Kao Li Ho, Gong, and Corkscrew—were now all dead. And apparently from the same cause, a fatal octopus bite. Maculotoxin.

What was going on?

"Occam's Razor," I said.

"What's that?"

"You know, the Occam guy."

"I know who he is, Finn. I'm the one who told you about him."

"The simplest explanation is usually the right one," I said.

"Correct."

"Well, if Occam were here, he'd say that the person who poisoned those pirates was the *only* person who could have poisoned them."

"Blue Jade?" he asked.

"Yup. She's the only one who has full-time twenty-four/seven access to the cooler room. And if anyone saw her with those little monsters, no one would question her. And have you noticed that they don't seem to affect her?"

"No, I hadn't noticed," said Uncle Stop.

I told him about the pirate queen handling the *zhangyu* after Kao had bit the deck.

"She picked them up?" Uncle Stoppard said, astonished. "With her bare hands?"

"Didn't bat an eyelash," I said. "What do you think it means?"

"Maybe she's immune to their poison," he said.

"Maybe she's part octopus."

"Why would she kill her own men?" asked Uncle Stoppard.

"That's the tricky part," I said. "But I'll bet it has something to do with the island. Or the *Manta*."

"So Blue Jade was creeping around her own ship, killing her own men with the octopi."

"I have another theory," I said. "I think she didn't use an octopus."

"But you said—"

"I think she used the octopus water," I replied. "*Danger Below* said that water could become contaminated, or poisoned, from the blue-rings."

"Envenomation," he said.

"That's the word. I'll bet Blue Jade poisoned those guys by injecting them with water from the coolers. Or with poison she extracted from the creatures. And if she had a supply of the stuff in her room, it wouldn't matter if the room to the octopuses was locked or not."

See? Occam's Razor.

"She'd use a hypodermic," said Uncle Stoppard.

Hypodermics are skinny. The wounds we saw looked bigger than a needle point. Of course, an octopus beak would be bigger.

"It would be easy to jab someone with a needle without getting caught," said Uncle Stop. "In fact, a killer in one of Agatha Christie's books uses that method."

"I think Mona used that, too." I said.

"I'm sure she did," said Uncle Stoppard. "Considering how unoriginal she is."

"Maybe Blue Jade got the idea from Mona. The pirates all seem to read her stuff."

Uncle Stoppard snorted.

"Why would she—Blue Jade, I mean—secretly kill those guys?" I said. "She can do whatever she wants. This is her ship."

"It must be an awfully big secret," said Uncle Stoppard. "Something so big that if her men ever found out, she would be in serious hot water."

"What do you keep secret from a pirate?" I asked.

"Treasure," he said.

A giant treasure. I thought about the voice I heard when I lay gasping on the deck of the ship after my dive. *This book'll make more money than Mona Trafalgar-Squeer's ever did.* What was so valuable about that techie book?

"If we can prove that Blue Jade killed those guys," I said, "we could start a mutiny."

"A mutiny?"

"They'd be so busy fighting each other, they wouldn't notice us slipping over the side of the ship. Borrowing an oxygen tank."

"We're back to the escape plan, are we?"

"Why not?" I cried.

"All right. Then let's prove Blue Jade was up to her eyeballs in these murders. How do we do it, Finn?"

"Simple," I said. "Slip into her room tonight, after she's asleep, and find that hypodermic needle."

15
SOCKS

"I have an even better plan," said Uncle Stoppard.

I had a bad feeling that his plan involved a skinny American boy squeezing his way into someplace he should not be seen squeezing.

"I'll be a decoy," said Uncle Stop.

Like a wooden duck?

Uncle Stoppard's new and improved plan was this: it was too dangerous to sneak into Blue Jade's room while she slept. Better to snoop around when the pirate queen was not there. So far, a good plan. Until I learned that I was the one who had to do the snooping.

"Why me?"

"You're smaller and lighter," he said. "It's easier for you to find places to hide."

True. Uncle Stoppard was more than six feet, and he was not the most graceful guy on the planet. The bruises on his forehead were the latest proof.

"How will you do the decoying?" I asked.

"I'll tell Blue Jade I'm worried about Foofy and Missy."

"The *zhangyu*?"

"I'll tell her that you and I have heard rumors that someone's tampering with their food."

"She'll blow up," I said. "She'll order the whole crew out on the deck and start looking for the guilty party."

"I'll stress that it's only a rumor. That I don't want to point fingers and get the wrong people in trouble. I think she'll appreciate that. Then I'll ask if she could accompany me to the coolers, we could look for signs of tampering."

"She would probably do that," I agreed.

"Which will give you time to search her room," he said.

"That's not a lot of time," I said. "You think she'll believe you?"

"Those blue-rings are the only things she cares about," he said. "I'm positive she'll want to check it out."

"I hope so."

"While she and I are talking downstairs," he said, "you slip into her room upstairs and look for evidence." Downstairs and upstairs. I was about to tell Uncle Stoppard that what he meant to say was *topside* and *belowdecks,* but then he added, "Come to think of it, maybe we could radio for help."

"How?"

"Blue Jade must have a radio in her quarters. And I noticed a VSAT on the tower of the ship."

"What's a VSAT?" I asked.

"Very Small Aperture Terminal. Like a small satellite dish."

"Why didn't you say satellite dish?"

"It's not the same thing," said Uncle Stoppard.

"But it would give Blue Jade access to global positioning systems and the Internet and all kinds of communications."

"I'll look for a radio, then," I said.

"Or computer," said Uncle Stop. "But the main thing is that hypodermic needle."

"Hypo, right. So, when do you start decoying?" I asked.

"Right after dinner."

Right after dinner never came. The pirates celebrated late that night. It was closer to 22:00 hours when we were taken back to the galley for recleaning. A fresh layer of uncooked noodles carpeted the floor. Uncle Stop asked our new guard (since our previous guards had both died) if he would tell Blue Jade that we needed to talk with her right away. The guard was sleepy and growly, but Uncle Stop said that the pirate queen was expecting our message. When the guard left, I slipped out of the room, darted down the hall, and hid in our closet cell. Our Pengo-less closet. I waited until I heard the massive steps of Blue Jade, her jewelry jingling, enter the hallway and disappear through the galley door.

I crept quietly down the hall and skittered up the steps. I reached the pilothouse without anyone stopping me. The pirates were in their cabins. I heard a radio playing country-western music behind one of the doors downstairs. Lots of laughter and cursing coming from others. Someone was losing another bet.

Didn't anyone keep a lookout during the night? Or was Clown Turtle Island so remote from the usual fishing and shipping lanes around the Barrier Reef that Blue Jade wasn't concerned about being surprised or attacked or arrested?

If I were a pirate, I would worry about the police each day. The sky-blue hull of the pirates' ship helped conceal them from a quick, unobservant glance. But the camouflage only worked during the day. How did the pirates stay out of jail? They carried those guns and rifles for a reason.

The pilothouse was a single room, large, windowed, and full of light. A king-size, or rather queen-size cot, lay in a corner. Captain Stryke had his own separate bedroom on the *Forty-Niner*. His stateroom he called it. Why did Blue Jade prefer sleeping up here instead of in some fancy quarters down below? Maybe because here she was always in control. The front of the pilothouse, facing the bow of the ship, was covered with dials, lights, intercoms, knobs, switches, and the steering wheel. There was the radio. And next to it a computer terminal with a modem. Blue Jade could jump up from her cot in the middle of the night and be ready for action.

I hoped she didn't decide to jump up here before I finished my search and sneaked out of there. She and Uncle Stoppard must be examining the coolers by now. If the King Bee caught me messing with her things, my bare arm would end up in one of those coolers as octopus bait.

Evidence. I needed to find evidence. Then I could try radioing, or computering, for help.

Hey, what was that black, square blob on the table next to the cot? I crept closer. The book, *Manta Technical Specifications*. This was the treasure that had sent me into that creepy nest of moray eels.

It wasn't evidence, though. It did not prove that Blue Jade killed her own men.

I started pulling out drawers and looking through cupboards. That's what the cops and detectives always did on TV. They didn't always know exactly what they were looking for, either. Not until they found it.

Good thing the pirates hadn't asked me to return their flashlight. Now I used it to scan the contents of Blue Jade's closets and shelves, sticking my nose into each dark corner.

Wow! Uncle Stoppard was a genius. I was checking out the drawers on the other side of the cot, opposite the tech book. In the first drawer I yanked open lay a plastic bag full of hypodermic syringes. Just as he predicted. And next to the bag lay a wrinkled, well-thumbed paperback, *Danger Below*. I was not surprised to see the pages dog-eared at the section on blue-ringed octopi. The word *maculotoxin* was underlined.

The second drawer held a large red hardcover. A physician's book on poisons. Let me guess. Yeah, she had the section on maculotoxin folded open. Whole paragraphs were underlined and highlighted with a yellow pen.

Why did she do it?

I looked across the cot at the tech book. Were those men dead because of the sunken *Manta*? Which reminds me, where was Billy Pengo all this time?

A voice behind me, outside the pilothouse windows. Someone was walking toward the door. I knew it, there was a lookout!

I grabbed several syringes, blue plastic caps covering their thin, deadly needles, and carefully stuffed them into a pocket of my shorts. I hoped Uncle Stoppard was right about me finding an easy hiding place.

I was fast, but not original. I dived under the cot, hoping the blanket and sheets that hung over the edge would conceal me from the approaching figure. I scrunched close to the wall, where it was darker.

The door opened. A man's shoes and legs walked past the cot. The socks looked familiar. Sandy-colored. Yikes, he sat on the cot. I bent my head, my bones hardened into coral. I stopped breathing.

The cot creaked under the man's weight. He shifted, leaning toward one of the cabinets. Was he talking to himself?

"Here we go," he said.

I saw his hand open the nearby cabinet and pull out an amber bottle. Liquor. The cabinet door slapped shut, and the cot creaked again as he shifted back.

Creak.

Now what was he doing? Ah, he was reaching for the *Manta* book. I heard him flip the book onto the canvas of the cot directly above my head. He riffled through the pages and laughed. Not so much a laugh as a deep chuckle.

I knew that chuckle. I had first heard it in the dark closet that had been our cell belowdecks. And those sandy-colored socks clinched it.

Billy Pengo.

He had given Blue Jade the location of the *Manta.* Now he was enjoying his freedom on the ship. Blue

Jade probably treated him as a friend; he certainly knew where the liquor was kept. So why didn't she kill him, as she had killed others? She had the book and knew where the ship lay. *Qing Bi* and her crew could salvage valuable equipment from the *Manta* and sell it: radios, radar, engines, pumps. But for some reason, Billy Pengo was important to her alive.

16
INTO THE COFFIN

Billy Pengo and Blue Jade were partners.

The pirate queen had learned about the *Manta* and the location of the technical manual from Billy. I could easily imagine him bargaining with Blue Jade as soon as he was taken aboard their vessel. He would give her information in return for his safety. What could Blue Jade do with the *Manta* buried down there? The stealth ship was too valuable to leave buried in the coral reef. The Ackerbergs would pay a big-time reward to learn its whereabouts. People would kill each other for a big enough reward. Look at television game shows.

Blue Jade had killed the other men for the reward money? That didn't make sense. If that was her reason for murder, she would have to wipe out her entire blue-bandannaed crew. Unless only a few other pirates knew about the *Manta*.

But her divers? No, the other divers were fishing for elephant pearls.

Perhaps a few pirates had overheard Billy Pengo talking with Blue Jade about the stealth ship. And if Blue Jade found out who they were, well then . . .

Let's see. The only pirates to die were Kao Li Ho, Gong, and Corkscrew. The three guys I had met on the island. They were buddies. If one of them heard about the *Manta,* I'll bet he would have told his friends.

Uncle Stoppard and I had wondered why Blue Jade would keep her killing a secret. Now I knew. If the other pirates learned her secret, learned that she and Pengo were planning on making their fortunes somehow from the sunken *Manta,* she'd have to kill all of them.

It *was* like a game show. The first person—or pirate—to reach the Ackerbergs would reap the reward. Blue Jade obviously did not want to split the money with her crew. Splitting it with one other person was hard enough for someone like her. In fact, if I were Billy Pengo, I'd watch my back. And wear needle-proof armor.

Those needles . . . the wounds on Gong and Corkscrew appeared too large to be made by a hypodermic syringe. On the other hand, I didn't get a good look at the needles yet. Blue Jade was a giant. Maybe she used giant-sized weapons.

Billy Pengo still sat on the cot, reading through the manual, drinking from the amber bottle. The same manual that I had—

Uh-oh. I was a witness, too. What would keep him from bumping me and Uncle Stoppard off, too? When I finally reached Reversal Island and told my story to my parents, and then to the authorities, the name Billy Pengo would be on my lips.

If Pengo had his way, my lips would soon be purple. To match those of Dr. Carpenter and the pirate trio. I was a threat to him. I would be able to prove that he was a traitor to the scientific community. He would lose his job, probably get arrested. Certainly for being an accessory to murder.

Too bad a tiger shark hadn't gotten him when the *Manta* sank.

That's something else. Billy lied to me. He said that lighting struck the ship and broke the hull. Water rushed in and sank them. But when Yelo and I dived down to the *Manta* earlier that day, the hull was a seamless wall of black metal. I didn't see any damage on the ship. Not a window was broken.

The *Manta* was sunk on purpose.

The Ackerbergs would be furious. If I could reach them first, tell them what really happened. Maybe they would be so grateful, they would help my parents and me return from Reversal Island. Months ago, after reading the skeleton clues in Iceland, I was convinced that the Ackerbergers were behind this second disappearance of my parents. The mysterious Institute seemed intent on shooting my parents all over the globe on unexplained archeological digs. Agualar and Tquuli among them. I was sure they were also behind my parents' "relocation" to the Great Barrier Reef.

If I told them about Billy Pengo's scheme to sell the ship's location—and her black box—to Blue Jade, I knew they would reward me somehow. Free my parents from their current job and let us go home.

That's what I would use the computer for. No one on the planet knew where the Ackerberg Institute was located, but there *was* a Web site.

Creeaak!

Billy Pengo was moving. I heard him stretch across the cot, and saw the canvas sag under his weight, an inch from my forehead. The metal cot legs strained with added tension.

A drawer opened, followed by a fumbling, crunching sound. He was grabbing a needle from the plastic bag! His white sneakers lowered to the floor and took the pressure of his full weight, the soft sides of the shoes puffed outward from his flexing feet. He stopped, and I saw one knee touch the floor.

He was going to lift up the sheet and look under the cot.

I backed farther into the shadows, imagining I was a ball of dust. I waited for the scar on his forehead to appear under the canvas. Another rustling sound. He must be digging through drawers, looking for something.

Pop!

A blue needle cap hit the floor next to his knee. Billy Pengo was preparing a hypodermic. Blue Jade had sent him here to prepare the maculotoxin for her next victim.

His knee knocked the cap and it rolled under the bed. Please leave it alone. You don't need it anyway, I begged silently.

The knee rose out of sight. The white sneakers shuffled toward the front of the pilothouse and stood there for a second. Staring out the window, I imagine. Thinking about the poison. The sneakers and socks traveled toward the door and disappeared.

I took a breath.

Uncle Stoppard was in danger. I was, too, but at

least I was aware of it. Uncle Stop was alone in a room with a killer. A killer with her favorite blue murder weapons swimming near at hand. If Blue Jade was indeed immune to the slimy *zhangyu*, all she had to do was lift Mittens or Fluffy out of a cooler. Or force Uncle Stoppard's arm into one. I had to warn him.

But I also had to contact the Ackerbergers. Tell them about the *Manta* and ask for their help. I looked across the room at the computer. In a few seconds I could start it up and send an e-mail to the Institute. But in a few seconds Uncle Stoppard could be poisoned. I knew how fast that maculotoxin worked.

I slithered out from under the cot and crawled to the door. Pengo was gone.

No one on that ship ever climbed down the deck ladder as fast as I did then. I don't think my feet touched a single rung. Two bounds carried me toward the hatchway. A crack of light showed the cooler room door was slightly ajar.

A dull silver light caught the corner of my eye. Moonlight gleamed off a metal object lying near the port gunwale. It was the only weapon in sight. I grabbed the air tank with both hands, then barged my way into the cooler room.

Blue Jade was standing behind Uncle Stoppard. He was looking down into one of the coolers. One thrust of her arm and Uncle Stop's arm would end up as a tidbit for Fluffy.

I couldn't stop to think. I had to save him.

All my strength went into that blow. I crashed the air tank into Blue Jade's shoulders. An ugly grunt tore through her throat. She swiveled her massive torso to stare at me as she sank to her knees. Her head crashed backward against Uncle Stoppard, throwing him against the cooler. Dirty water sloshed over the sides and spilled onto the floor. Poisonous water.

"Don't touch it!" I cried.

"Finn! What are you doing?" shouted Uncle Stoppard.

Blue Jade mumbled something. Chinese? Tagalog? Octopus?

Her eyes rolled back into her head as she pulled a dagger from her boot. A wicked piece of sharp metal that glittered like gold and curved like a serpent's back. I had seen that dagger somewhere before!

"Kris," she said. "My kris . . . your blood . . ."

The few words I could make out did not sound like good news. I threw the air tank at Uncle Stoppard. "This is yours," I said, panting. "We have to escape."

He staggered under the sudden weight of the tank. "What? Now?"

"He's after us," I said. "She is, too."

"Blue Jade?"

Blue Jade was lying on the floor, waving her dagger weakly in the air. Her eyes closed, and the blade dropped with a clang.

"Her and Billy Pengo. Quick, we have to go now!" I stooped over and picked up the dagger. We had no other weapon.

"Did you see Pengo?" said Uncle Stop.

"Hurry, before they hear us."

"Finn, wait. Look at her ears."

Ears? Her ears looked fine. "We have to go now," I said.

I ran out on the deck. The capped hypodermic needles weighed down one of my pockets, while the flashlight banged around inside the other. I stuffed the dagger through a belt loop.

Uncle Stoppard looked over the gunwale into the dark water. "We'll have to buddy up on this tank," he said. "It'll take a few minutes to find the other one you left down there."

"Just go," I said.

Then I saw a shadowy shape through the hatchway. Eyebrows. Fang appeared suddenly behind him. We were doomed.

Eyebrows raced toward us, then suddenly stopped. He turned to his pal Fang and said calmly, "Twenty rinngits the big one hits the water first."

"Forty rinngits, and I say it's the boy," said Fang.

"Splash or no splash?" said Eyebrows, lighting a cigarette.

Billy Pengo rushed onto the deck behind the pirates.

Unless you're an Olympic diver, it's hard not to splash. Uncle Stoppard and I crashed through the water together, tangled in a cocoon of bubbles. His hand grabbed my head and forced the mouthpiece into my face. I sucked in a quart of air and returned the air hose.

I followed Uncle Stoppard's example and positioned myself vertically in the water, legs together. We sank like stones. The flashlight was not powerful. Luckily, the water around the Great Barrier Reef was crystal clear. Dark, but clear.

Trading off the tank's mouthpiece, we reached the coral coffin in less than a minute. I led Uncle Stoppard around the underside of the black hull. The cavern leading to the open porthole bristled with shadows. It looked smaller than before. The cavern, I mean. The porthole looked farther away, a black hole at the other end of a watery universe.

A school of turtles glided across the mouth of the coral cave, blinking in the beam of the flashlight. I recognized them as clown turtles, the white eyes and red-tipped beaks.

I pointed toward the porthole.

That's the one, I signaled to Uncle Stoppard.

He gave me the hose for one more gulp of air, then gave me an encouraging pat on the back. Gee, the sunburn on my neck hurt even underwater.

I aimed the beam directly ahead of me as I half-swam, half-crawled through the orange cave. I was more conscious than ever of the poison carried inside the coral's hard surfaces. I tucked my legs in close to each other. A cut or scrape could make a person sick. This was not the time for extra problems.

I glided nearer to the porthole.

I wondered if the floater I saw down here earlier, the dead man from the pilot room, was drifting near the porthole. If I saw his head in the flashlight beam, that would be like the scene from *Jaws* all right.

There *was* a head on the other side of the open porthole. Not a human head.

Two black eyes like evil raisins stared directly at

me. Below the eyes, a miniature cavern stuffed full of razor-sharp incisors pulsed and throbbed. Were moray eels nocturnal creatures? I should have read further in *Danger Be—*

The thought was only halfway through my brain when twelve feet of yellow muscle and a head full of teeth lunged through the porthole.

17
BLOOD IN THE WATER

The moray's bullet head skimmed above my hair. I rotated in the dark water and saw the eel turn, coil itself like a monstrous mattress spring, and gather itself for another attack. The jaws gaped wide. My flashlight beam glittered off a hundred fangs.

The eel shot forward like a sprung rubberband. I closed my eyes. Again, the gross yellow serpent glided above my head. Uncle Stoppard was pointing frantically at the flashlight. The eel's beady eyeballs were being blinded by the unfamiliar beam.

I aimed the light directly at the creature's head. The eye's reflected the pale white light. The eel seemed uncertain. It slowly wriggled through the coral arms, averting its face from my beam. It lay between me and Uncle Stoppard. And Uncle Stoppard had the air tank.

I was feeling light-headed. I needed oxygen.

I waited until the eel swam round a coral arm, out of my sight. Then I swam rapidly toward the porthole, stretched my arms into an arrow point, and paddled my feet like a hunting dog. In a second I was through. The air tank lay just below the porthole where I had dropped it. I chewed onto the mouth-piece. The oxygen filled my lungs and cleared the cobwebs from my brain.

I trained the beam quickly around me. No floaters, no morays.

Now Uncle Stoppard and I each had our own air tanks. We could swim all the way to Reversal Island. But how would we find it? I hadn't planned on us escaping during the night. Darkness made it harder to find our way. In the daylight we would be able to see the pirate ship hull. Filtered sunlight would show us where the island beaches sloped down into the water. We could pick our way around Clown Turtle Island, then strike out through the ocean toward Reversal Island. Mom and Dad were a mile or so away. But in which direction?

What we needed was a compass.

Hey!

I looked through the porthole and saw Uncle Stoppard peering in. The moray eel must have found another creature to terrorize. I shined the light on my face to get Uncle Stop's attention and held up a finger. It was the universal sign for, "Wait a minute, I'll be right back."

Uncle Stoppard shook his head—the universal sign for "No way, forget it,"—but I swam away, pretending not to see him. Remembering Blue Jade's crude map for finding the pilot room, I navigated the dark halls and retraced my former steps. Former fins, I mean. Yup, there was the friendless, abandoned sneaker. And up ahead, there was my goal. The floater.

Sorry, but I needed his watch more than he did.

The guy floated near a corner of the ceiling, actually a former wall of the lopsided *Manta,* gently bumping his head against the metal surface. I reached for his arm ·and pulled off the thick watch. Yeah, the digital display was still running. The compass was intact, too.

Back at the porthole, Uncle Stoppard helped pull me through.

Drat! There was that moray again. He swam into view as I reentered the coral cave. A second snake had joined him. No, a thin red line, more like a ribbon, threaded its way past my face. It curled like a red trail of smoke.

Uncle Stoppard pointed again. This time at my leg. Looking down, I saw the red ribbon spiraling slowly from a gash on my left leg. A sharp straight wound. The *kris!* Blue Jade had slashed at me with her dagger. The dagger that now dangled from my belt loop. In the excitement, I hadn't realized she actually wounded me.

Blood attracted the moray. Two of his buddies were still inside the *Manta.* How long would it take them to sense me bleeding nearby?

Sharks were attracted to human blood as well.

Uncle Stoppard grabbed my arm and pulled me away from the sunken ship. All we could do now was swim to Reversal Island as quickly as possible. At a safe distance from the coral coffin, I noticed Uncle Stoppard staring at my leg. He ripped the waist of his T-shirt and pulled off a handful of green fabric. Wrapped around my leg a few times, it made a pretty good bandage. At least I didn't see the red ribbon gushing out like an oil well. A few bloody bubbles, however, did escape as we continued to swim.

I was swimming with a dagger at my belt and a pocket loaded with tiny hypodermic harpoons, and I was worried about—

Harpoons! That was it. That was how Corkscrew and Gong had been killed. And maybe Jocasta Carpenter, too. If I was right, Uncle Stoppard and I were extremely lucky that we hadn't already been murdered. Several times we had only been a few feet away from the killer, and from the silent murder weapon.

I showed Uncle Stop the compass. He nodded his head and smiled. We gauged our direction and headed directly west. As soon as we were back on land, I would explain to Uncle Stop what I had discovered about the killer.

Gosh! If I was right about the murder weapon, then there was only one person who could be the murderer. Occam's Razor again.

The pirate ship must be close overhead. I didn't want to risk aiming the flashlight in an upward direction to find it and get our bearings. Blue Jade and Billy Pengo would see the light and get a fix on our location.

We kept swimming west. I figured that after an hour of swimming we could rise to the surface. Slowly this time, of course, and exhaling the whole way. The dazzling Pacific moon and stars might shed some light on Reversal Island. Or on Clown Turtle Island, so we'd know where *not* to swim. How would we distinguish the two isles at night?

According to the floater's watch, we had been

swimming for, let's see, fifty-five minutes. Everything looks the same at night underwater. If we hadn't had the compass, there would be no way to tell we had traveled at all. The *Manta* might pop up in our flashlight beam in the next second.

I trained the beam around us, seeing if I could notice any difference in the seafloor. Maybe spot the beginning of a beach rising below us.

A shadow trailed behind us. Long, dark, moving gracefully. A tiger shark.

I glanced down at my leg. Uncle Stoppard's homemade bandage was soaked with my blood. A red thread twirled away, leading into the dark waters behind us. It made the perfect dinner bell for any nearby shark.

I shot a look at Uncle Stoppard. I could tell from his expression, his crinkly green eyes, that he had also seen the sleek shadow. He jerked his head forward. Nothing to do but swim.

He pointed a finger upward.

"Surface," he bubbled.

Exhaling, I reached the surface without a pain. The stars were like searchlights compared to the unlit waters down below.

Oh, no, the pirate ship was only thirty yards away. We had been swimming in a gigantic circle around that stupid turtle island.

"Look at the mast," said Uncle Stoppard. Mast? The pirate ship didn't have a mast. Neither did this ship. It was the *Forty-Niner*. After looting it, shooting Captain Stryke, and capturing Uncle Stoppard, the pirates had abandoned it. Not their problem, I guess.

"Hurry," I said. Sharks can swim a lot faster than humans can.

I looked behind me only once. No telltale fin sheered through the surface of the dark waves. That didn't mean that Jaws wasn't right below our feet.

Uncle Stoppard and I swam toward the stern of the *Forty-Niner.* Her gunwale was lowest at that point and would be the easiest place to board her.

Thirty yards away, then twenty yards.

Something crested through the water at my back. I heard the sound of waves and splashing several yards behind me.

"Faster, Finn!" yelled Uncle Stoppard.

Ten yards . . . five yards . . .

We gained the *Forty-Niner*'s stern and pulled ourselves aboard. Just in time. As I stepped onto the familiar red-and-gold deck, I saw a rubber-suited shadow at our backs climb swiftly over the gunwale. A diver in fins, goggles, and air tank. A gloved finger on the trigger of a speargun.

18
CONE OF DEATH

Without shifting the speargun, the diver threw off his goggles and ripped off the rubber hood.

"Billy Pengo!" cried Uncle Stoppard.

Billy shrugged out of his knapsack and tossed it onto the deck. "Stoppard," he said. He lowered the speargun.

"The pirates were after me as soon as you two escaped," he continued.

"Where were you hiding?" Uncle Stoppard asked.

"Not hiding," said Billy Pengo. "They had me in another cabin. Torturing me."

Yeah, drinking Blue Jade's liquor in her cabin must have been real torture.

"Those pirates kept asking me about the *Manta*," said Billy.

"Too late," I said.

"That's what I learned, mate," said Billy. "You went down there. Into the ship."

"Blue Jade asked me," I said.

"Did you get a good look at her hull?" he asked.

"All angles and sharp lines," I said.

Billy nodded. "A stealth ship. Like the stealth bombers. Undetectable by radar."

"Whales don't really have radar," I said.

"You're right," said Billy. "It's more like sonar, isn't it?"

"Ships have sonar, too," I said. "Especially ships like navy submarines or coast guard ships." Anyone in authority, I figured.

"Smart lad," said Billy, with a grin.

"That's why Blue Jade wanted the *Manta,* right?" I said. "Not because there was anything valuable on the ship. But because of the ship itself."

"The technology," said Billy. "Other people would pay a high price for that kind of advanced weaponry."

"It's not a weapon," I said.

"Not yet," said Billy. "Oh, Stoppard. Would you mind handing me my cigarettes from that bag?"

"Sure," said Uncle Stop.

"They're inside one of those pockets."

"NO!" I shouted. I kicked the knapsack across the deck, out of Uncle Stoppard's reach. He gave me a serious frown. Billy sat down on the gunwale and chuckled.

"You've a smart boy there, Stoppard," said Billy. "He just saved your life."

"My life?"

"For the time being, anyway," added Billy. This time he wasn't grinning.

Uncle Stoppard looked puzzled. "But what was in—?"

"The murder weapon," I said. "It's how Corkscrew was killed. And Gong. And maybe Dr. Carpenter, too."

"No, Dr. Carpenter was smothered," said Billy.

"How can you be sure?" I asked.

"Because I did it," said Billy. "Simple really. She had swum ashore and was resting on the beach. Exhausted. She was too weak to put up a fight. I figured it would look as if she had drowned. And it would have . . . but not to you, Finn."

Billy had been there on the beach.

"So you got to the island first," I said.

"I was prepared," said Billy. "I knew how long it would take the *Manta* to sink once I opened the ballast tanks. I did it at night, I figured the others would be surprised and not be able to get to safety."

I remembered the floater with the stain on his shirt.

"Did you have to shoot that guy in the pilot room?" I asked.

"You saw Dr. Martin? Yes, he caught me at the controls. It was during the outburst. I didn't think anyone would hear the gunshot in the storm, but then it really wouldn't matter, would it?"

"I don't understand why you did all this," said Uncle Stoppard. "And what is in that knapsack?"

"The murder weapon," I said. "A geography cone."

"What's that?" asked Uncle Stop.

"A cone shell. I saw it on the beach on Clown Turtle Island."

"That's what gave me the idea," said Billy. "I had lost my gun during the sinking of the ship. But I knew those cone shells carried enough venom to knock off several people. And I needed a weapon."

"It shoots a stinger at its victims," I explained to Uncle Stoppard. "Like a harpoon. And it would make a wound like the ones we found on Gong and Corkscrew. Bigger than a needle mark, but smaller than a bite."

"And its poison would affect people differently than the blue-rings," said Uncle Stoppard.

"It doesn't kill that quickly," said Billy.

"That's why Gong was found in the hallway," I said. "And that's why we could talk to Corkscrew minutes after he had been jabbed by that thing."

"The geography cone's poison can take up to thirty minutes before it kills you," said Billy.

We had been wrong the whole time about the blue-ringed octopi. It was confusing with so many poisonous creatures living in one area. The details of how the octopi got in and out of a locked room, or how they actually attacked Gong and Corkscrew, had thrown us off the real killer's trail. If only we had thought about Occam and his razor earlier. The geography cone popped back into my memory while underwater when I remembered the hypodermic needles in my pocket. They reminded me of harpoons. And *harpoon* was the word Billy Pengo used to describe the cone's deadly stinger.

"I told Gong I had some cash in my bag," said Billy. "When he got stung, I said it must have been a pin stuck in there. And when he didn't find any cash, I blamed the other pirates for nabbing it first."

The night air was warm, but my clothes were wet. All three of us were dripping onto the deck. "What about Corkscrew?" I said.

"Corky was asking me about the *Manta*," said

Billy. "He already heard me and *Qing Bi* talking about it. He wanted in on the action. When I was taken back to the closet, I held the bag up, next to his back. He never knew what it was."

"You were already planning on selling Blue Jade the information about the *Manta,*" I said.

"Not originally," he said. "I was going to give it to someone else."

Someone else?

"You always intended to steal the ship, didn't you?" said Uncle Stoppard.

Billy Pengo smiled. "I joined the *Manta* in Hawaii. Her first navigator didn't get sick. That was a result of poison as well. I had to get on the ship somehow. It was all part of the plan."

"So who was going to buy the ship?" I asked.

"I was going to keep it myself," said Billy. "And give it to a group of friends. Friends of the earth. Oh, that's not their name. You'd know it if you heard it. But you wouldn't realize that they have a whole branch devoted to covert operations. Eco-terrorists, you'd probably call them."

"You killed people in order to save the planet?"

"It's people who are killing the planet," said Billy. "Just look at the coral reefs. Look at your own American cities with air pollution, noise pollution, toxic waste dumps. Oil spills every year, each spill worse than the one before. If a few people aren't killed for the good of this earth, then all of us are going to die."

"So why give the ship to Blue Jade?" I said.

"I didn't," said Billy. "It was just a measure to save my life. *Qing Bi* had no way to salvage the *Manta.* But that ignorant pirate was stupid enough to think that someone would pay her for the technical manual and the location of the ship."

"They won't?"

"It would cost as much to raise the *Manta* as it would to build another one. I thought I could sink the ship and retrieve her. I planned on getting to the mainland in a lifeboat. I didn't know that blasted coral was under there. The coral ripped my lifeboat as I passed the island back there. "

"So, the scientists and crew all died for nothing," said Uncle Stoppard.

"In a war there are casualties," said Billy Pengo, with a shrug.

Uncle Stoppard asked, "And Gong was killed because—?"

"I couldn't take a chance," said Billy. "Kao and Gong and Corky were good pals. When you two blokes were off cleaning the kitchen, Gong and Corky came in and took me to *Qing Bi.* She knew that I had come from some kind of ship. And she was looking for plunder. When she heard it was the *Manta,* I thought she was going to kiss me. She knew all about the ship. She told me she followed it on the Internet.

"I worried about those other pirates listening in on our conversation. And I was right—when Corky came back to pull me out of the closet and question me some more, it proved he had heard what was going on. Gong was killed as a precaution. If no one learns that I had a hand in sinking the *Manta,* it all goes down as a tragic accident."

Billy raised the speargun. He aimed it at Uncle Stoppard's chest.

"This is a precaution, too," he said.

A small explosion boomed at my ear.

"Uncle Stoppard!" I yelled.

Spearguns don't make noise. Billy Pengo's air tank had sprung a leak. Pressurized air shot from the tank like a retro rocket. Billy was shoved backward onto the deck. The speargun flew from his hand. Escaping air spun him around the floor of the deck—is floor the right terminology?—like a pinwheel firecracker. Billy's head struck a chest built into the gunwale and knocked him out. The tank kept hissing.

"Captain Stryke!" exclaimed Uncle Stoppard.

The captain pulled himself wearily up the hatchway. A pistol hung from his right hand.

"Good thing I kept this," he said. "I came out to Australia for peace and quiet, and I'm gonna get it."

"But, Captain," said Uncle Stoppard.

"Yes, Mr. Sterling?"

"You were dead, you know."

"Was I?"

"Shot," I said. "Uncle Stoppard saw you."

"What did you actually see?" said the captain.

"Well, I saw that Corkscrew guy raise his gun and fire," said Uncle Stop. "You were standing behind me. Then I heard you cry out and fall overboard."

"An old trick," said Captain Stryke. "That twisty guy never even touched me. His bullet flew past my ear with inches to spare."

Maybe his bullets were twisty, too.

"I fell into the water to escape the pirates," said the captain. Like Uncle Stoppard's plan back on the pirate ship. "After they left, taking you with them I figured, since I didn't see your corpse up here, I climbed back onboard and tried to fix that blasted radio."

"No luck?" I asked.

"Don't worry," said Captain Stryke. "I never leave port without telling my pal Jim Fairburn, the harbormaster, my schedule. If I'm not back there in three days, which is yesterday, I believe, he'll try to get me on the radio. And if that doesn't work, Jim'll send help."

"Look out!" yelled Uncle Stoppard.

Billy Pengo had gotten to his knees. He steadied himself and grabbed the speargun.

"Aaaahhhhhh!" he screamed and grabbed his hand. He looked at me with a sick light in his eyes.

He had steadied himself by holding on to his backpack. I could guess that he touched something inside the pack. The geography cone had struck again.

Billy climbed onto the gunwhale.

"Stop!" I yelled.

Uncle Stoppard held me back as Billy slipped over the side of the *Forty-Niner.* A single splash, and then the night grew silent again. We must have stared at the dark water for more than an hour without speaking, watching for a sign, a bubble, that Billy would return to the surface. Nada.

"It's better that way," said Captain Stryke. "Let that coward die in the ocean since he loved it so much."

"We have to get to the island," I said. "Reversal Island."

"We need to return to the mainland," said Uncle Stoppard.

"You mean *that* island, Finn?" said the captain.

I followed his pointing finger. A low island lay only a hundred yards off the starboard side. Palm trees stood out like dark shadows against the darker background of the western sky. The sun would soon be up.

"Have you seen the lights again, Captain?" I asked.

"No more lights," he said. "I was going to swim over there in the morning, but—"

I jumped over the side of the *Forty-Niner* and started to swim.

19
GREAT BARRIER

A hundred yards of ocean was nothing compared to the distances I'd traveled through water in the last few days. It seemed only a minute had passed, and I had reached the island. Just like the moment I arrived on the island of the clown turtles, I made landfall during morning light. A warm breeze stirred the leafy golden tops of the trees. The sky became a vast bowl of pale, fiery pinkness.

"Mom! Dad!" I ran up the shore and into the forest of Reversal Island.

Because I had hurried to save Uncle Stoppard from the poisonous clutches of Blue Jade, I had missed using the pirate queen's computer to reach the Ackerberg Institute. No matter. After I told my parents about the *Manta* and Billy Pengo, we could tell the Ackerbergers together. I was sure they had some way of reaching their mysterious employers.

"Dad!"

A few strides through the coconut and mango forest brought me to a large, sandy clearing. The clearing was empty except for two mounds of rocks, one at the far end of the clearing, one in the center.

The clump of rocks at the edge of the clearing hemmed in the whaler's legendary and lifesaving well. The center mound was covered with ashes, burnt sticks, and empty beer cans. An old campfire. I recognized the beer cans as the same kind that Uncle Stoppard and I picked up in the galley of the pirate ship.

Nothing else.

I ran past the well and into the forest on the opposite side. Blue water glittered like cold jewels beyond the mango trees. I could already see the ocean on the other side of the island. Reversal Island truly was a dot on the map. It was smaller than Clown Turtle Island, no bigger than a football field. In less than five minutes I had circled the entire island, walking the shoreline until I ran into Uncle Stoppard and Captain Stryke, who were stepping out of a small boat onto the wet sand.

"There aren't even any birds here," I said.

"I'm sorry, Finn," said Uncle Stoppard.

"You found nothing?" asked Captain Stryke.

"I found out what was causing those weird lights we saw, Captain. A bunch of drunk pirates having a wienie roast."

"Ah, lanterns," said the captain, nodding to himself.

"Come on, Finn," said Uncle Stoppard. "I just got here. Let's keep looking."

"Why? It's no use. Nobody's here. And if the pirates had seen them—"

"They would have said something, yeah."

I don't understand. The skeletons had told us to come here. *Mikill veggur,* they said. *Mikill veggur.* Big wall. Great barrier. Different words for the same thing. Blue Jade and *Qing Bi.* Or did the same words mean two different things?

What else would fit those blasted Icelandic words? Suddenly I felt incredibly tired. The trees and sand and waves looked boring and sad. The bright October sky gave me a headache.

"Perhaps they're on a different island," suggested Uncle Stop. "Maybe we got the L-word wrong."

"Yeah, wrong."

"Let's look at Captain Stryke's charts for other *L* names."

Yeah. Okay. Why the H.E. double hockey sticks not?

I lifted my weary feet into Captain Stryke's rubber lifeboat and sat down. He started the motor, and we began puttering our way back to the damaged *Forty-Niner.* I shaded my tired eyes from the rising sun and stared at the yellow bottom of the rubber boat.

"I don't believe it," moaned Uncle Stoppard.

"What?"

"Your friends are back," said Captain Stryke.

A sky-blue boat was approaching us from the east. Blue Jade's ship was on a collision course with our own.

"She'll ram us!" cried Captain Stryke.

Who cares, I thought.

"No, no, she's slowing down," said Uncle Stoppard.

"If I have to clean that kitchen one more time ..." I said.

The pirate ship drew alongside our little rubber

craft. Pirate faces peered down at us from the rail of the deck. But no gun or rifle barrels. The pirate faces parted in the middle, and a giant shadow stepped forward.

"Little Turtle," said Blue Jade. "You are a crazy boy to fight with Blue Jade."

"Uh, it was nothing personal, your honor. I mean, I thought you were trying to poison Uncle Stoppard."

"Your *jiujiu?*" she said. Blue Jade laughed. "You are a crazy boy or a brave boy. Maybe both. Did your friend Billy find you?"

"He's no friend of ours," said Uncle Stoppard.

"And no friend of mine," said Blue Jade. "He tried to sell me that stupid ship. Who would be so foolish to buy a sunken ship?"

"But you wanted that book," I said. "That technical manual I found for you."

"Thank you, Little Turtle," said Blue Jade. "You did me a great service. But it was not the book I was after. Nor the sleeping *Manta.*"

"But the book—"

"I have no quarrel with you or your *jiujiu,*" said Blue Jade. "I am one who knows how to show her gratitude. Your ship is damaged. I will radio for help once we have left these waters."

"Billy Pengo is dead," I said.

"Is he?" said Blue Jade, lifting an eyebrow. "Did you kill him?"

"He was killed by the same thing that killed your men," said Uncle Stoppard.

"Poison," said Blue Jade.

Then I explained about the geography cone and how Billy kept it hidden in his backpack.

"Yes, the pretty little *ke* is deadly," said Blue Jade. "Small things can be very dangerous. Here, for you, Little Turtle." She whipped her hand and a dark object flung through the air. It landed with a soft thud on the rubber bottom of the boat.

"I believe the Immortals watch over you, mystery writer," said Blue Jade. "Perhaps because you already know so much about death."

"But why did you make me go through all that trouble finding that book for you?" I asked.

"Not the book," said Blue Jade. "The box."

The black box?

She lifted a box up to the railing and tipped its lid. She pulled out a gleaming golden knife, like the knife she wore in her boot. The pirate queen smiled. "There are three of them." The golden knives! It was part of the treasure that the *Manta* crew had found in the Hawaiian islands, the treasure from the ancient Indonesian kingdom.

"The knives of Srivijaya!" I cried.

"I follow the Internet, too," said Blue Jade. "Billy Pengo did not know what I was after. I did not trust him. Since he betrayed his friends, who would he not betray? I pretended it was the book I wanted. But I always kept my eye on those knives. From watching the *Manta* cameras, I knew where the knives were kept each day. The mission of the *Manta* is very educational."

Billy probably wasn't that interested in the Srivijaya knives since they were discovered *before* he joined the crew in Hawaii, and since his interests were more ecological than cultural.

Then the pirate queen waved. "Say hello to

Mona Trafalgar-Squeer for me," she said. She turned from the railing and vanished. The blue ship pulled away and streamed eastward.

"Did you notice her ears again, Finn?"

"I noticed she always wear blue earrings."

"No, those are her ears."

"Her ears are blue?" asked the captain.

"She has blue rings on her lobes, like the octopi."

I thought she had been wearing blue earrings to match all her other jewelry.

"I think she's been giving herself small doses of that maculotoxin over the years," said Uncle Stoppard. "Eventually she would build up an immunity and maybe even turn her ears blue. It's only a theory, but it would be the only logical way she could handle Fluffy or Mittens without being poisoned herself."

"You mean Floofy and—oh, uh, never mind."

Giving herself injections of toxin would explain the drawer full of needles and the big book of poisons.

"Forget the woman's ears!" said Captain Stryke. "What's in the package?"

Dark blue tissue paper covered a hard, heavy object.

"A turtle," I said. "A blue jade turtle."

"Wow. That must come from her own collection," said Uncle Stoppard.

"There's an inscription underneath," I said. "Can you read it?"

"Looks Chinese," said Captain Stryke. "Probably something like 'Good Fortune' or 'Happiness and Long Life.'"

"Don't ask me, Finn," said Uncle Stoppard. "The only Chinese I know is from the menu of the Great Wall of China."

The Great Wall is the best Chinese restaurant in Minneapolis. Uncle Stoppard and I have gone there a dozen—

Wait a minute. Great Wall?

Those Icelandic words again. *Mikill* and *veggur.* They could mean *great barrier* or *great wall.*

"Ah, that's it!" I said.

"What, Finn?"

"Ah!"

"Ah?"

"The Icelandic rune that Mom wrote on the skeleton. It stood for *A* or the 'ah' sound, right?"

"Right. *Ah.*"

"And where did she write the *Ah*?"

"On the skeleton's mandible," said Uncle Stoppard.

"What's a mandible?" asked the captain.

"Chin," I said. "Chin. Get it? Chin ah. Chin ah?" China!

Mom had created a rebus puzzle on the skeleton's chin. She knew that Uncle Stoppard and I would figure it out since we both love solving puzzles.

And where else was there a Great Wall but in China?

"The Great Wall," Uncle Stoppard murmured. His cucumber-green eyes glazed over with a faraway gleam.

I looked at the small jade turtle in my hand. None of us could read the inscription carved into the blue stone, but to my eyes it spelled good luck.

A NOTE FROM
STOPPARD STERLING

The *Conus geographus,* or geography cone (also
called geographer cone), is a gastropod, an ocean-
dwelling, salt-water-loving, fish-eating killer snail
which lurks inside a beautiful shell the size of an
average adult human's hand. The glossy shells are
banded in gold, brown, or pink against a bright,
creamy background. The *geographus,* a small, slow
beast, and no match for bigger and faster predators,
makes up for its lack of size and speed with a gut full
of deadly venom. *Geographus* detects the presence
of fish by siphoning water through its slimy body and
using chemical receptors like microscopic noses to
sniff the water particles for traces of fishy fin and
scale. When it finds a suitable prey, the *geographus*
launches a tiny harpoon, filled with venom-bearing
teeth. The fish becomes almost instantly paralyzed
by the potent poison. The harpoon, gripping the
motionless fish, is reeled in, coneward, by a thin
thread. Dinner is served.

More than thirty humans have died at the hand,

or harpoon, of the geography cone. One young American Marine stationed in Guam discovered two cones on the beach and decided to pose with them for a photo. He did not know what they were. The Marine held them up on either side of his head, the two cones each launched a harpoon in the young's man neck, and he was dead within a minute. An Australian diver found a cone and placed it inside a thick nylon bag. The cone's harpoon pierced through the bag and stung the diver in the chest. Within twenty minutes he grew dizzy and had difficulty breathing. The reaction time varies with each victim.

If you should happen to be stung by one of these creatures, apply pressure immediately. Sometimes artificial respiration is required. There is no antidote for the venom.

If you should happen to be captured by pirates, on the other hand, be patient. Eventually they will show a weakness or flaw which can aid you in forming your escape plan. They are not nearly as deadly as cone shells. Nor as intelligent.